Buttered

Biscuits

Buttered Biscuits

Short Stories from the South

Cynthia Boiter

Muddy Ford Press
Chapin, South Carolina

FIRST EDITION.

Cover art by Thomas Crouch.

Library of Congress Control Number: 2012938437

ISBN: 978-0-9838544-0-1

CONTENTS

DEDICATION

When I was growing up, rarely did a morning pass that I did not wake up to the smell of biscuits baking in my mother's oven. My father and brothers ate them the same way my mother made them – like a sacrament. Sometimes they were smothered in gravy; others, sticky with molasses. I liked mine with butter.

My mother's hands touched every molecule in the make-up of the biscuits she served our family. And while her biscuits, like those of a lot of Southern women from her era, baked up light as a feather, they were heavy with meaning.

Pride, purpose, love.

I never served homemade biscuits to my family like my mother did for hers. But, I do have something to give them that is equally filled with meaning.

Pride, purpose, love.

To Annie, Bonnie, and Bob, thank you for pushing me to put this collection of stories together. I finally did it. Here's my pan of buttered biscuits. They're dedicated to you.

INTRODUCTION

or

How to Make a Pan of Buttered Biscuits

In your mother's chipped yellow bowl – the one she made biscuits in every morning when you were growing up – sift your flour until it rises to a soft peak. Scoop out a little hole, or indentation, in the middle of the flour and reach into the Crisco can and draw up a generous handful of shortening. Pour several splashes of sweet milk into the hole in the flour, then add your shortening and work the mixture with your hand, squeeze it between your fingers, until it is the right consistency to knead.

Put the ball of dough on the floured cotton cloth you laid out before you started – the one you'll fold up when you're through and store in the chipped yellow bowl like always. Now knead it, but not too much. When the dough is right, get out your old maple rolling pin with the broken handle, rub it good with flour, and use it to roll out your dough until it's about as thick as a pancake.

Eyeball your dough to make sure there's enough, then use your biscuit cutter – the aluminum one with the wooden handle that's just a little warped – to cut your dough into circles that you'll arrange in rows on that old black pan.

Bake until done.

Being careful not to burn your fingers, use a knife to slice each hot biscuit open and slide a square of butter inside. Leave the biscuits on the pan so they'll stay warm and the butter will melt.

When you're ready, serve your biscuits on that old blue platter – the one that's the color of your daddy's eyes.

Buttered Biscuits

Mary Anne

It was so cold sitting in the pick-up truck that I just about couldn't feel my toes anymore. My teeth had gone past chattering to jumping, so I clenched my jaw tight and that set my whole head to trembling, just like those tired old brown leaves clinging to the scrub oaks outside my momma and daddy's house. Just like me they were hanging there, shaking, wanting to let go, but afraid to fall.

It was quiet under those November stars, with the wind barely whistling through the doors of the truck and the tree limbs coughing as they pushed and tugged at each other above us. It was too cold for crickets. Next thing I knew, Avery reached over with that big old arm of his and slid me across the cracked leather seat of his truck to where our thighs almost touched and the gearshift banged hard against my knee. He didn't mean it to hurt. With my knee still smarting and the back of my legs burning from the cold of the seat, he gave me a kiss. At first, it scared me like I don't know what. It was a lot rougher than I'd always thought a kiss would be. Pretty soon though, my mouth softened up and it got easy and nice and I could feel myself start melting away. Before I knew it, I found myself kissing that man back, and me, who never in my life kissed a soul who wasn't in my family, well, I was feeling fine.

But my head was full.

It was really going to happen and I was going to let it.

1

It was just like being born all over again. The world was about to turn on over and be sweet because, I, Mary Anne Lane, was about to become Mrs. Avery Watson and any minute now I would walk right into that house right there and tell my momma and daddy that it was so.

Nothing else in the world mattered. All the sack-cloth dresses and knotty rubber bands I'd worn in my hair; they didn't mean a thing. Always being last to bathe my body in a tub of dirty, lukewarm, been-used water didn't matter at all. I didn't even care about not going to the Sweethearts Dance, even though the boys in my class had picked me as their princess. Who knows, I just might've won, if I'd a had a dress that amounted to something and Daddy'd let me out the door. But none of that mattered. The world was new and fresh, and I was never gonna sweep a dirt yard again in my life.

I felt like I could breathe.

Avery got out on his side of the truck and stood there for what seemed like forever before he came around to get me. When he opened the door and put his hands around my waist to lift me off the seat, it must have been a month before my feet ever touched the ground. He made me feel dainty and precious, like Doris Day. He was Prince Charming and I was Cinderella and that 1949 black Ford pick-up was my pumpkin carriage. I didn't even mind that Momma had left her spit jar on the front porch steps. We just walked over it like it was a bug on a log. And, when the door to the house didn't want to open because the rain swelled it up so, Avery leaned his big shoulder against the stubborn wood and pushed, and slew that dragon right then and there. He was strong.

The heat from the wood stove parched dry our faces as soon as we got inside, and there wasn't a lamp lit in the house. But I could hear Doreen and Peggy giggling in the other room. They weren't asleep, but they were playing like it so Daddy wouldn't fuss and Momma wouldn't cry. Little pockets of sage and dressing and turkey smells still hung in the corners of the kitchen. Momma had left a plate on the

2

table with slices of fried fatback, baked sweet potatoes, greasy with lard, and two pieces of corn bread on it. Avery saw it, once't our eyes got used to the dark, and reached over and grabbed himself a piece of bread. I didn't want to say anything, but I knew Momma and Daddy would both a'thought that was too familiar of him to be doing.

Momma had only seen him three or four times before. One Sunday afternoon he was waiting on our front porch when we walked up from church. I could see him sitting there from way on down the road, a long time before he saw us a'coming. He'd brought me a handful of petunias he'd picked from his granny's yard and for Momma, he'd brought a sack full of scuppernongs that grew down by Tobe's Lake.

"How do, Mr. Lane, sir," he'd said, reaching for Daddy's hand.

"Miz Lane," he said, holding out the sack.

We sat on the steps and watched ants crawl in and out of hickory nuts while, in the house, Daddy slept in his chair with the batting hanging out of it, and Momma and the girls fixed Sunday dinner. I kept waiting on them to call me in to come do my share, but they let us alone pretty much. Except Doreen and Peggy kept peeking out the window and making kissy noises. When I heard Momma's chipped blue plates bang down on the table and the chicken stop sizzling on the stove, I told him it was time for me to go in.

He stood there in the yard, whistling and fidgeting, with one foot on the stoop and the other planted firm in the clay, while I ran a pint mason jar full of water for the flowers. Momma looked at me over the pan of green beans she was dumping into a bowl and said through her teeth, "Was you wanting that boy to eat Sunday dinner with us?"

"No, Momma," I whispered, dried clay clinging to the back of my throat. "He's just a boy."

I started putting the biscuits on a platter, burning my fingers with every one, and dropping them so the flour from the tops flew like mist in the air.

3

I didn't dare look out the window to see if he was still out there, but when I heard Doreen say, "there he goes," I glanced over once.

He was walking up the road with his hands stuffed down in his pockets, kicking stones every step of the way. It was funny the way the sight of him made me feel. Not entirely good. He could just as well have eaten with us. Would've been glad to have eaten with us. Momma would've been glad to have him, mostly 'cause Daddy would've had to behave. But I reckon I felt a little pleased, too, not to have let him in. And a little bit scared, to see him walk up the road by himself, not knowing for sure whether he'd walk back down it again or not.

Another time, we had all rode into Greer to get tobacco for Daddy, and buttons for some dresses Momma was making. There he was, and Lord, he looked fine, walking across the street with a paper bag in his left hand and a Coca-Cola in his right. He had on this pale green summer shirt with blue stitching along the collar, and his sleeves were rolled up high on his arms. He had a pack of cigarettes, Lucky Strikes, tucked in his pocket next to a blue fountain pen, the same color as the stitching on his shirt. The same color as his eyes. My heart about stuck to the back of my chest and I could feel the heat crawl up my neck toward my face. My ears burnt red. I was scared to death Daddy was going to see, and I didn't know what he'd do if he did.

But it was Momma who saw. She looked at me, then she looked at Avery, then she looked back at me for a long time. I couldn't read her face, to save my life. Then she sent me back into the remnant shop with a nickel for a spool of white thread and, when I got back, Daddy was talking to some men about a tractor and Avery was nowhere in sight.

Five months later, there we stood in my momma's kitchen, him eating corn bread and me feeling like it was Christmas morning and afraid to look under the tree. There might be a bag of nuts, or there might be a pair of socks, but

4

there hadn't ever been no china doll under the tree for me.

I lit the lamp on the table and the room took on a glow. Momma's homemade curtains, bleached almost to pink, fluttered as the heat moved through the house. Light bounced off the wire of the pie safe and made it sparkle like silver threads. The deep green glasses set on the shelf above the icebox caught the same light, like emeralds, and I swear, they glowed, too. I poured Avery a cup of buttermilk and he turned it up and drank it without a breath. I quick wiped out the cup, dried it on a towel, and put it away.

"Well," he finally said, taking in a breath and looking at me all matter-of-fact. "Let's do it."

The faucet dripped into a worn black pool in the bottom of Momma's cast iron sink. Four, five, six times.

"What we gonna do?" I finally said and tossed my chin up like I wasn't sure what he was talking about.

"Well," he said again, looking out the window over the sink into pitch darkness that went on and on. "You think you're gonna be able to spend the rest of your life with me, or not?"

I had to blink the tears out of my eyes right then and there. See, my momma loved me and she showed it whenever she could. But my daddy didn't give a flip for none of us, and most of the time, he didn't seem to care much about Momma neither. All I knew of a daddy, of my momma's husband, was fussing and drinking and sleeping and, one time, he told me that if I didn't have a good head of hair, I'd be ugly as a bird.

So here's this good-lookin' man, with a decent job at the mill and a bought-and-paid-for truck, reaching under the hair laying on my shoulder and holding the back of my neck with the softest, sweetest hand, next to my momma's, I'd ever known. His nails were clean, and his skin was smooth, and he smelled like something other than gin or sweat. Puddled in his eyes were two little pools of tears shining scared in the light of the lamp and, Lord have mercy, I'd've been a fool not to have loved him, too.

5

But I was no fool.

I knew good and well that every man who ever walked either beat his wife or he didn't. As far as I knew then, drunkenness was as much a way of life as visiting the cemetery come the first Sunday of the month, and eating new potatoes in May. Still, I was a girl and girls don't want to bother with worries like that. Even though they were what kept me most company when I lay in my bed at night.

The girls had gotten quiet, Daddy was snoring, and the faucet still dripped.

It could be, I caught myself thinking. I moved closer so I could stand by him on the rag rug, still wet from supper dishes. Looking down, I could make out pieces of aprons and overalls and baby dresses woven into it, and little whiffs of ammonia floated up from our feet. Maybe a man could make a living and eat his wife's biscuits and not raise the first hand to her. I'd heard that kind of talk from the preacher and some of the girls at school. It might be that money could be in the bank, and flowers grow in the yard, and blessings be said before a meal. Drinking might be nothing more than a little something out of a jar on a cold dove field.

I caught myself thinking.

The first few drops of rain plinked down on Momma and Daddy's tin roof and I took in the smell of washed dust as it drifted up from the cracks in the floor.

It could be so.

But not even forty-five years ago, young as I was and as much as I'd'a given anything to, never would I have ventured a wish or a prayer of how good it really could be. That nightfall could bring whispers not to wake the babies, and touching feet, when it was too hot to curl up in bed. Wrinkled hands, rubbing knots out of stooped old, garden-weary shoulders. Flowers on my kitchen table. And looks from blue eyes that could go so deep into my soul they'd draw up fists full of memories and sore places and sweetness so fine it'd bring a lump to my throat in the middle of the day. And even now as I remember his face, gone these many years. Never would I have guessed. It was the kind of thing only angels could tell.

By then, the rain was pouring a steady song on the roof. I felt light in my limbs, like my elbows could float and pick me up off the world. So, I took hold of his hand and let go of whatever breath I had left of my own, and we walked into the little hall where Momma kept her ironing board set up. Cases of empty Coke bottles were stacked on the floor. With the third knuckle of his middle finger on the hand I wasn't holding., Avery tapped three times on Momma and Daddy's bedroom door.

"Mr. Lane, can I have a word with you, sir?"
My toes were still numb.

Aunt Priss

Aunt Priss was one of those girls to whom, at the painfully tender age of twelve, nature had come early. She had a fullness about her, both body and face, which caused women to whisper and men to murmur whenever she passed by. Priss was profoundly aware of the newness and the wholeness she had come to possess, but had long since mentally filed this sensation away into the burgeoning collection of everyday things she deemed miraculous.

But it wasn't miracles Priss was shopping for on that scorched July afternoon when my grandmother sent her down the narrow dirt road that ultimately connected their home place to the spot where Leonard Putty had long ago built his country store. Her momma had been specific: baking powder for biscuits, a box of salt, and washing powder to do a week's worth of wash as soon as she got home. As she walked, sack in hand, back toward the curiously rambling house in the grove where she lived, the length of her blond braid, tied up with a red grosgrain ribbon that had come in the toe of a Christmas stocking, bounced off the small of her back like the beat of a young man's heart.

The road was thin and would have been muddy had there been even a drop of rain in the foothills within the month. There wasn't a farm in Duff's Bridge that did not suffer and shrink that summer, and if it hadn't been for the

9

generosity of old folks and distant cousins with tiny kitchen gardens they could water from their wells, many a large family would have gone hungry, save for the peas they had put by in the spring when the ground was still wet from winter's snow.

Priss herself had ventured out on a January Saturday morning to help scatter seeds through the shallow dust of snow that had fallen the night before. She watched in wonder week by week as the baby seedlings emerged, first little more than a poke beaming out of the ground. Soft and new grass green that made her mouth water but, wise as she was, she knew not even to touch the tender leaves lest she damage them, ruin them, disrupt the plan.

Instead, she held her hands gently around the sprouts, hoping to somehow send her warmth and prayers to them when she visited the pea patch on cold afternoons after school. They bloomed pink and white when the mornings were still cold. The vines tore through the air, grasping for support at the knotty cotton strings her daddy had tied and posted in the patch.

And when the buds first appeared and Aunt Priss saw them and let herself ever so gently touch the swell within the soft safe folds, she felt the hot, wet salt that welled under her eyes and behind her nose. And she knew most assuredly that there were miracles all around and within her. It mattered not if anyone else saw the miracles for what they were. It was the miracles that made the tingle in her soul. And more the pity that her momma, my grandmother, saw the peas as something only to be seasoned with black pepper, fatback, and salt, and had no sense of the magic she stirred in her pot. But the peas filled their stomachs fresh in April and May, then from thick glass jars for those dry summer suppers.

As it was, the yellow straws of grass and weeds, encroaching on the wheel paths and narrowing the lane even more, scratched at the backs of Priss's knees above the once white socks that covered her shins. Her flowery dress, a salad mixture of greens and yellows with pearly buttons down the front, had once belonged to her own mother. It took them both by surprise the morning in June when she slid it over her head to play dress up with her sisters, only to find that the hem hit her just below the knee, the elastic of the sleeves neatly above her elbow, and the placket came together with little room underneath for play clothes of her own. That night, my grandmother hung the dress, laundered with starch and pressed smooth with a hot flat iron, on a three penny nail on the back of the girls' bedroom door, and it was what Priss wore on the first and every third day of school come fall.

The boy leaning in front of Putty's country store had never seen Priss or the flowery dress before she walked out of the store's screen door and past the tiny box of a concrete block building that served as the community's post office. At sixteen, he had long since quit school to work his daddy's farm, tire of that, move to Duff's Bridge to be the man of his widowed aunt's house, then leave her alone, needy and worried, that very day to smoke cigarettes and take up space in front of Putty's store. More man, or what could be a man, than boy, Wallace had little on his mind that day, and was free to let his thoughts linger on my Aunt Priss as she took the familiar path toward her home in the lush green woods with a confidence that caught in his throat, like the dust on his shoes.

Drops of sweat had gathered around the boy's collar and across his lip, and the slight morning breeze that passed with Priss made him feel cooler and fresher than he'd felt in a long time. The crispness of the cotton and the waft of talc which followed the girl like trails of dandelion seed in the air only added to his sense of a strange newness. He felt the need to breathe a little deeper, stand a bit taller. And he did, with a spine almost straight. He watched her gait as she moved from rut to rut, the sack dangling from her freckled arm, loose and casual. Wallace approximated my aunt's age at fourteen, but no more, or she would have noticed him when she left the store. Judging by the neatness of her hair,

11

by how clean she smelled, he figured her to be one of those girls from a fine family, a well-off family. Wallace had no way of knowing that the road she traveled on led only deeper and deeper into forests and foothills and then the Great Smoky Mountains after it left the parcel of dirt Aunt Priss's daddy farmed. In his mind, he saw the girl, who strolled to the store only for the sake of leisure or pleasure, approach a large white columned house where lush flowers bloomed in well-tended gardens despite the paucity of rain. He envisioned her gliding through the air on a front lawn swing, her hair loosened from its braid, her face a portrait he captured from his mind since he'd seen only her back as she'd walked away from the store. He thought of her daddy, and how the daddy might look at the daughter, as his prize, his possession. Rich old men, even those who truly loved their daughters as their children, still used them as examples of all that they had, and all they could have, Wallace judged. The daughter, the girl, even as the essence of the daddy's restraint, was still a messenger to the world, a taunt to men and boys like Wallace.

Flicking the remnants of his cigarette into the sand, the boy sniffed, dug his hands into his pockets, glanced back at Putty hunched behind the counter over the thick store ledger, then moved one slick soled shoe before the other along the same path Priss had taken.

Her footprints were there, right in front of him, indentations in the black dust marking her trail. Slowly, he matched his pace to hers, shortening his stride and marveling at how small her gait seemed. He hopped back and forth, from rut to rut and inhaled deeply, searching for the scent of soap and talc and, when he thought he had caught it, holding his chest still to try to trap the fragrance there. Holding it and holding it. He thought he might explode.

Breathing again, he quickened his pace when he noticed that the girl was nowhere in sight and a canopy of hardwoods now shaded the road. The road had become more of a trail, then the trail a path. The grass that grew between the ruts, hungry, determined to live, grew greener now nurtured by the moisture from the shade of the blue ash trees, and the ruts all but disappeared into the now taller weeds interspersed with toadstools and mosses that spread before him on the forest floor.

He scanned the shadows of the hardwood trees and peered through the traces of the cedars that lined the path, and quickened his pace to try to catch up to the place where he figured my Aunt Priss might be walking. Might be running by now, he thought, and he visualized the look of her, the energy, romping along the path like a mustang at full gallop, but playful and full of herself, the blond braid whipping through the air.

Perspiration dappled his back and his breath began to catch as his ill-used arms and legs tired from the trot. Her scent was lost in the earthy essence of the forest. Mosquitoes, quickened by the shade, buzzed past his ears like bullets, and sweat bees smacked into his face. The blood pounded in his temples, and he slowed and bent forward, face red and stinging, resting his hands on his knees, and waited on his breath to return. He coughed and spat.

The wind rustled the skirt of Aunt Priss's dress against the dull grey bark of a sweet gum tree, and Wallace squinted until he found her, a frozen silhouette against the blanket of the woods and the undergrowth of hardy saplings strong enough to endure through both tender winter and thirsty summer. The sun was too high for a shadow to meddle with, and Priss was bathed in the bits of light that passed through the branches above her. She, too, was bent at the waist, wrists outwardly curved with the weight of her upper body resting on the front of her thighs.

Her elbows extended from her sides like wings.

Priss didn't see the boy behind her, nor did she hear his labored breath. Though not forty yards away and his chest heaving noisily with a mixture of exhilaration and fatigue, she didn't detect his presence or his intrusion upon the safety of her woods. With attention so deliberate, so focused, Priss was caught up in the convergence of all her energy into the study of a scene at the base of the sweet gum. There, amid the meandering roots and dusty Earth lay the scrawny, almost lifeless body of a baby, a mammal, hardly breathing, hardly out of a mother's womb. The fall from the tree, though cushioned by years of mulched leaves and lichens and grasses, as well as several thick inches of soft, dry soil beneath that, had stunned the foundling and delivered it an even greater shock than that of its brutal new home above. As Priss stared in a comfortable state of awe, the numb little body, all fuzz and flesh, quivered and struggled as if, as much as it wanted to live, it was terrified that it would.

Priss smiled.

Wallace could see only the shape of her body. Her shoulders were hunched and her back curved like an old woman's. His breathing steadier now, he watched as she squatted on her haunches and laid the sack by her knees on the ground. He couldn't take his eyes off the smooth, slim line of her back and the bow tied neatly at the base of it. He gripped his right fist, lengthened his thumb and imagined using it to trace the ordered ridge of her spine from her neck all the way down to the bow. The perfect little bow. He studied her as she leaned forward, her knees near the ground, her seat on her heels, the tails of the grosgrain ribbon the only connection between the girl and the grass of the Earth. He wanted to know what would make her kneel there. And he wanted to see her face.

Wallace felt a shiver as sweat trickled down the backs of his legs to behind his knees. He waited, watching Priss, charmed by the stillness and the needing to know what she was doing. Needing to know Priss. Tanager, Warbler and Wren chattered in the trees above him, and Wallace could hear nothing but the throb of his heart in his head.

Then in a movement much like an early morning stretch and yawn, the girl's arms reached out into the air at her sides, palms up and open, long translucent fingers spread wide. Her shoulders rose slowly, almost meeting the lobes of her ears as her arms arched upward and her head lay back. Her face was ecstatic. It was bright and clean, and it was pointed toward the sky. And Wallace could see it. Wallace could see the face of my Aunt Priss.

There was nothing to stop the boy. His legs moved before he knew they were going to, and he sprang toward the girl, grasses and saplings slapping at his thighs and knees, his ankles turning over in the holes of rotted roots and pain shooting up through his bones like lightning splintering wood. Priss did not move. Her up stretched arms formed a V in the air and the boy raced toward her. Her tiny charge writhed on the ground before her, and the boy ran on. Her eyes squeezed shut against the glint of the sun that gaped through the trees and he came, and he ran, until nothing but the air could make him stop. He caught the scent that he had so wanted to know in a current of wind that swirled between the boy and the girl, and he opened his mouth to taste it. It was sweet. He closed his mouth and inhaled deeply. Thunder erupted above, but the taste in his mouth was sweet and it was clean and it was good. The boy stopped.

A deer, lithe and fragile, but not frightened, effortlessly appeared from behind a stand of yellow birch trees, froze, caught Wallace's eyes and peered deep into them. Clouds began to form overhead.

Rising and turning to look at the boy, Priss saw him for the very first time.

"Hello," she said.

The first few drops of a warm summer rain dotted the boy's shirt.

And the ground beneath the sweet gum tree, save for a slight mussing of the mosses where the body had been, was bare.

15

Toby and Bess

The tomatoes smelled green to Bess. They looked ripe; choke berry red and firm, and the skin gave beneath the striated nail of her thumb like there might be juice bubbling inside. But when she held the blossom end to her nose and inhaled deeply, waiting for the scratchy, sweet-acid aroma of ripe tomato peel, all she got was the scent of cool water and wax. The tomatoes smelled green.

"Toby," she declared to her husband who had moved on to a display of Chilean grapes and fuzzy green kiwi in a basket. "I've been wanting a good tomato sandwich for such a time now." Her voice, though cracking and splintering into lost syllables in places, spoke melodiously of the rich southern earth she'd grown up in. Had grown old in. Her hair, long strands of palladium twine, was plaited and knotted and anchored at her neck.

Toby left the cart and shuffled back to Bess's side. He took the tomato, now mashed and weepy, nestled it among the other produce, and pulled a wrinkled handkerchief from his pocket to wipe the juice from Bess's freckled hand. Holding his wife by a brittle wrist, her arm the fragile tendril of a morning glory vine, he guided her through the lettuces and cabbages, purple with a mingling of green and white, and back to the buggy where their groceries waited.

He pushed on.

"Davie loves a good tomato sandwich," Bess smiled

to the air, her mind aloft on a memory, snowy lashes fluttering soft over wrinkles on peach-veined cheeks.

The shiny back of Toby's head nodded at her.

Her first born, Davie was tall and thin like his daddy. A hard worker and always the first in line, he had a mighty appetite that brought him early to his momma's supper table and kept him there long.

"Mayonnaise and Sunbeam ... salt and pepper. He likes a fair amount of salt and pepper ..." Bess's thoughts traveled on and Toby had learned to let them wonder until they found a familiar place to light.

Determinedly, he chose a pre-tied bundle of purple grapes, tested one between his thumb and forefinger, put them in the cart and shoved. Lagging behind, Bess let her fingertips drag along a sandy row of melons and with her lily brow pinched into a befuddled ridge, pressed at a window of cellophane covering a cantaloupe sliced in half for display.

She squeezed her eyes, shook her head quickly left to right and tried to clear the dew she felt gathering in her head.

Bruised bananas, picked-over peppers, over-ripe apples; the air around them carried the yeasty memory of fermentation and Toby took a deep, ripe breath of it and let it fill the vaults of his chest. Like a high wind tumbling in the top of a stand of windbreak pines, he could sense his wife's agitation as it mounted. As surely as he felt his own pulse in his fingertips, he knew that Bess's was gathering speed.

"I want you to know," Bess soon declared, facing her husband and shaking a crooked finger toward his chin, "that boy ate three whole sandwiches when he came in from the schoolhouse yesterday."

Toby pulled the handle of the cart to a stop. The tang of bulging grapefruit stung his nose and made him pucker.

"Three!" she cried. "Ate them as fast as I could fix them!"

She chuckled now; her high-noted laughter, an interval off from a tuning fork's tine, launched a familiar question that floated like mist between them. Hearing her own laughter, like a misguided bird darting about on a screened-in porch, she startled herself and clamped her hand to her mouth, trying to capture the noise of her voice.

Standing on the patched and pockmarked linoleum, Bess felt the aisles of produce draw back from around her. Strangers shifted faces then disappeared into a murky haze. The music from the speaker overhead, a song her boys had sung along with on the radio, played now without words and echoed in her ears.

Then, within the switch of a breath, she was there, calico apron tied in a bow, tending to her kitchen stove - stew beef simmering; okra frying in a pan; slices of sticky canta-loupe crescents waiting in a chipped ceramic bowl. Davie and Bud in shirt sleeves and crew cuts, talking and laughing noisily right outside the kitchen window, their heads buried under the hood of a sky blue convertible Chevrolet.

Toby looked deep into the hazy river of Bess's eyes and searched for the place where her mind had taken her. Nearby, a new mother pushed past with a cart, her baby boy gumming a slippery carrot, and a gray haired woman rubbed at the fuzz of a peach in her hand.

In Bess's kitchen, the radio's song was just a murmur beneath the banging of tools and the horseplay and rough-housing of little boys grown up into friends. Better watch the okra lest it turn black and tough, she reminded herself.

A stranger's voice boomed loud over the radio's music and spoke gibberish in her head. *Canned peas -- special price -- aisle eight.* Like a scent on a stubborn breeze, the kitchen was gone leaving Bess with the sugary perfume of melon in its own syrup and a bareness she couldn't name.

Bess felt the world stir beneath her faster than she could move. She tried to catch it – tried to pull her arms in close to her body and steady it; hold on to the place and the air she breathed. But the rush of the memory's vacuum caught her weightless and she gulped for air and pressed her

19

brain for an image to ground her. Another breath, another
room, another time. Two boys in navy blue – one red-eyed,
a marble pillar in a starched uniform, dried salt crusting his
chin; the other, lying cold in a coffin at his side.

There was no air left for Bess to breathe. Her gut
empty, she balled her fists onto her hips, shifted a stocking
foot in the heel of her canvas shoe and, angrily, desperately,
stomped.

A spray of tears washed across the woman's face,
the shiver of her chin putting Toby in mind of a newly born
blossom on a vine. Lifting her hand from her hip, he tucked
two fingers under the petit-point cuff of her wisteria sweater
and extracted a linty tissue which he placed, twisted and wad-
ded, into her knotted hand.

A teenaged stock boy sauntered by with crates of
lemons and pears.

Toby's bulky hands, unkempt and calloused and as
wrinkled as a summer sheet, wrapped around Bess's frail
ones. With a gentle force he pulled her toward him. Ignoring
the stock boy and the young mother and any other customer
who chose to look into his business, he pulled her toward him
and stepped into his wife's pain, letting the crest of her brittle
gray head nestle just under the curve of his chin.

And there they stood.

When the spell had passed, Bess looked up at the
man with a parchment paper smile, and gave him back to the
groceries. He turned her about and cradled her papery elbow
in his hand and thought of onions. Cousins to the lily, he
remembered. He thought of how the skin of the onion sepa-
rates and flakes, goes crispy at a touch and flutters away from
the bulb before the layers ever feel dry inside. Fresh herbs,
bundled into bouquets on ice, sent wafts of green and mint
and springtime into the air. Toby guided Bess back through
the okra and the squash to the place where the makings of a
Sunday dinner waited in a basket. They pushed on.

Precious

Precious was the only one of my babies with the eyes.
I bore me five children, three boys and two girls, but nary
had a one of them the eyes that Precious had. Set wide on
her face. And dark. Dark as burled walnut. Dark as Indian.
None of my other babies had any of the Cherokee blood in
them that ran so fierce in my momma's veins, and smolders
to this day in mine. They were always lily faced in winter and
peach pink come spring. Like their daddy. But Precious, I
believe she had the blood. I know she had the eyes.

From the first one on, my babies always came late.
Late in the year and late on me. David, Jr. was born one
cool September, a year to the day after his daddy and me had
married and moved into our little white-grey tenant house
with the pecan trees in the yard. Big ol' trees, even back then.
David, Sr. called me his mother-child. It's a fact, I wasn't
much more than a girl, barely seventeen-year-old and heaving
my belly around that summer. Down row after row of hard
field dirt, so full of rocks and stumps that the only thing that
wanted to grow was me and my baby.

Two years later, David, Jr. barely off the breast, Lee
Thomas was born on an early frost. I was hanging green
tomatoes up by their vines in the shed when my water broke
and soaked the dirt floor. I took a bucket of sand from
the yard and threw it over the wet spots, then went up on

21

the porch to rock and wait by a pot of faded pink petunias
I'd planted the spring before. I could smell a field burning
from way on down the road. It was near dusk when David,
Sr. came in from the fields and he took right off to fetch a
neighbor-lady to help with the birthing. Me and David, Jr. sat
on that porch the whole time, watching the sun climb and fall,
listening to the katydid songs, and waiting on Lee Thomas to
come.

The two of those boys kept me so busy back then
that Myra wasn't born till 1930, just a few days before Lee
Thomas turned six. She was frail and dainty. David, Sr.
would hold her little pink self in the palm of his hand on a
square of crazy quilt his Momma had started before she died.
Myra would lay there, soft and fine, looking like china, the
winter sun nearly shining clean through her skin. Her daddy
would've just as soon dropped off the face of the earth as
to have let anything happen to that child. I ironed her little
cotton dresses and pinned her little red curls, but it didn't
matter how much I wanted that little girl, or how much I
tried to make her mine. She wasn't born for me. She was his;
Daddy's girl, through and through.

Then, nearly five years after Myra, Albert came. Lee
Thomas and David, Jr. were bringing in a Christmas cedar,
bigger than both of them put together, the morning Albert
was born. I could hear Myra through the knotty pine walls
whining for her daddy, and him trying to make do in a kitchen
where he'd done little more than sat before. But, of course,
he went to her and patty-caked and hushed-little-baby'd, and
sure enough, she quieted down. So, Albert came to me alone.
And that was alright. He'd come from a wife's cold arms and
a man's rough hands and a late winter night that should've
been spring. I knew he'd be all there was for me, so I kept
him to myself for a while and kootchy-koo'd his little chin,
rubbing my hands over his satin belly and peach-fuzz head,
inspecting his little manhood. Like every one of them before
him, he was pink and quiet and blue-eyed, like his daddy.

And, even though I knew for a fact that it was so, nary a one of them ever looked like they belonged to me at all.

Maybe it was the spring rising up in me that made me make babies that time of year, then carry them so long until, when they finally came, both me and the earth were plum worn out. But somehow, late winter oft seemed to put me that way and, sure enough, I'd have another armful come Christmas. But it wasn't that way with Precious. I thought I was worn out before I even knew she was coming. But I was wrong.

It was the driest summer I believe I ever lived. The garden looked like it'd been planted in ground dug up from another part of the world and put where my dirt belonged. My sweet moist clay, what I'd worked egg shells and potato peels into for years to turn soft, lay just as dry as an old lady's powder. Corn stalks were bent and brown. My runner beans, once so bright and green like new grass in April, withered and wrinkled and clung to the very wire they were strung on.

David came into the kitchen in the middle of the afternoon, me slicing fatback and putting green beans on for supper. He stood at the chipped porcelain sink, took a jelly jar off the shelf, and sucked down cup after cup of cool well water, little dribbles slipping down his chin to his old plaid shirt. Then, he wiped his face with a red checked rag that streaked clean a swatch of pale, pink skin across his eyes and down his cheek to his neck. And for that bit of time, I could see the boy in David like he was seventeen-years-old. Hungry and alive. Full of himself. And me, standing there at that table where I'd made biscuits for over twenty-five years, I felt like that girl I used to be. Tall, lace petticoats, ribbons in my hair.

Something inside me made me go to him. I filled my arms and chest up with him from behind, and pulled down the collar of his old cotton shirt with my chin and tasted the sweat on his neck. I could smell the work in him, and when I ran my hands down his tight shoulders to his arms and then around to his belly, I could still feel the muscles just as hard and smooth as a melon, like they'd been years before. Years before when the bed was so cold on winter nights we could see our breath, but the warm we made between those thick quilted covers filled the entire house.

I don't know what came over me that afternoon. My hands were quaking like a web in the rain, and my chest was tight and heaving with breath that I just wanted to blow out of myself like skyrockets at the county fair. I remember hiking up the skirt of my pink gingham shift and sliding the inside of my thigh clear up to his hip pocket as he was standing there, looking almost afraid, but with cinders burning dark in his eyes. And his breath; it was heaving, too.

Then, he turned and kissed me. Kissed me like a little boy gives sugar to his granny; shy and self-conscious. But, not weak, no sir. Lifting me up off that worn heart pine wood floor like I was no more than a wisp of dry straw, he took me down the hall to our little room at the back of the house. I'd painted the walls pink the year Myra was born. He laid me down on Momma's cast iron bed next to a basket of clean overalls and sheets that should've been put away by then. I grabbed a' hold of the waist of his britches and pulled him down to me. The fresh clean smell of the sun and the wind in the clothes was so sweet I could taste it.

It'd been a long time since me and David had warmed a room, and I think that sweaty August afternoon was the first time I ever understood what all the fuss was about. I felt big and strong. Like I was glowing. And, it was me. I was the one doing it. Making the heat. Making the glow. David's eyes were wide as china saucers and I just danced around that man, touching him and having him touch me. It was like my fingers and toes were shooting off sparks and the insides of my arms and legs were throbbing with the sweetest pain I'd ever known. I took him like a man takes his bride. And with every push and pull, the top of my head just opened up wider and wider and out poured dishpans and dirty diapers and jar

24

after mason jar of put-by corn and peas and damson plum jelly. I let it all go. And, it took me with it.

Then, the house was quiet. Slowly, the call of whip-poorwills down by the woods' edge and tree frogs and crickets chirping to the dusk brought me up. Albert and Myra were fussing in the barn over chores. I smelled my beans, burnt and stuck on the stove, so I pulled on my shift and ran to the kitchen. The fatback was all runny and soft. David brought me my blue apron, laid it on the corner of the table where I made my sausages, then walked out the back door and toward the field where his plow sat idle. The screen door slammed behind him and I tied my apron back around my waist, then used its corner to wipe the sweat from my eyes. In the sky over the creek, I could tell it was coming up a cloud.

It turned rainy in September and Indian summer came on and stayed till late November. I dug me some sweet potatoes as fat and red as Rome apples. And perfect, not a scar on them. Holding my apron by the corners I filled it up so full and heavy until the smell of the dirt was thick in my nose and the small of my back ached with the weight of them so. Tomorrow's supper, I thought. But, as I laid them out on a careworn sheet to cure in the cool night air, I couldn't help myself. I picked out the fattest, smoothest one I could find, like I usually put aside for David, and slipped it bulging in the pocket of my shift. When I put the biscuits on for supper that night, I slid my secret, all covered with lard, into the oven beside my old, black bread pan. By the time the beans were soupy and the bread about brown, I was sitting guilty on a bucket in the pantry, eating me a steamy sweet potato, slicked down with butter, and scorching the roof the of my mouth with every bite I took.

That's when I felt her. There wasn't no sweet potato could make the bump in my belly like I felt then. Like a hunger, but without the empty. Like an itch in a spot you can't scratch, and you feel it there for a minute, then you feel it all

25

over you, and then it's gone. And you can't move. You can't even breathe until your body tells your brain and your brain tells your heart what it surely already knows. There's a baby in there. A baby, and it's strong. I was forty-three years old and I'd thought that I was done. But as I swallowed that last bite burning hot down my throat, all I could think was, there's more.

It rained the whole winter through. The tin roof leaked and the front windows stuck and I didn't think the earth would ever dry up. When it did, it left the smoothest green carpet of moss under the pecan trees that I'd ever seen in my life. Like a velvet cloth that ran over the roots to the edge of the woods and disappeared in the brambles. And like the buds on the berries there, I was big and swollen with something new.

I watched the strawberries come, all through April and into May. From blossoms to little green knobs that grew bigger and whiter till they were pink and finally peppered the patch on the other side of the barn with blood red berries that stretched down the hill and ended near the rocks at the creek. It was the second Sunday in May, and I was too big to go to church, so I sent David and the children on without me. I stood in the screen door, watching a house wren build her nest in the hydrangea by the porch, and waved until they disappeared down the road. Soon as they were out of sight, I got me a peck basket and headed for the patch. The dew was still on the berries and they were cool from the night. I'd wander along, pick me a ripe one for the basket, pop another one in my mouth. Pick one. Eat one. Pick one. Eat one. Pure joy.

I ate my fill and wound up, hot and worn out, by the creek. The sun beat down and I could feel my scalp turning pink and sore. I pulled the slippers off my swollen feet and stepped onto a smooth stone in the creek bed to let the water rush over my heels and toes, cold as ice. I just stood, waiting on the cold to travel up my legs to my belly and run a chill up and down my spine.

When the first pain hit, it squeezed me so hard that I knew I couldn't make it up the hill to the house. Each of my babies had come quicker than the last and Precious was about to come and come fast. I went to the shade of a pecan tree and squatted on the moss. It was soft under my toes and I reached out to stroke the nap with my hand. That's when another pain come. Hard. I caught my breath and hugged the trunk of the tree and didn't holler a single time, though I could taste salty blood around my teeth and on my lips. A cloud, perfect and puffy as cotton on the boll, moved slowly across the sky and shaded the sun off the berries and the creek and the trees. By the time it passed, Precious lay, wrapped in my blue spotted apron, on a soft basket bed of ruby ripe berries. She was long and gold, with skin like mine. Dark headed. Tiniest fingers you've ever seen. And Lord, those eyes. It was like looking in a mirror and seeing me and my momma and my baby all look back at me at once. Those eyes pulled my face right up to hers and bore into me as hard as summer rain bores thirsty soil. Talking to me. Talking to my soul. Telling me, "momma." Telling me, "baby." Telling me, "it's gonna be all right."

But I knew, as soon as I saw the gold going dull and her eyes start to falter, I knew that this little bit was all there was. All that was meant to be. She opened her mouth to cry, but not a sound come out. I patted her and patted her, but it wasn't any use. Her eyes got narrow and her little fingers turned nearly as blue as her daddy's eyes. No use at all. It wasn't supposed to last, I could tell. Just only long enough for me to see. She was mine, and I was hers. We belonged.

I'm not gonna say it didn't hurt. It was a pain worse than bringing any other one of my babies into the world ever brought me. Twice that. More. But, just like when I made her, it was a sweet, sweet pain. I'd seen her. I'd seen her eyes. I could let her go. So I lay her little cheek against my bare bosom and gently rocked her back and forth, back and forth,

27

rubbing the back of her head and feeling the fine silk of her hair twixt my fingers, until she just wasn't warm any more. Shakily, I laid her little body back in the basket and pulled the apron up to her chin. Then, I stretched my own long self out across the wet moss in the shade, and waited for the strength to move.

Dobie

Timbro Wallace was a practical man; a decent man who wanted nothing but peace for his wife, Dobie; nothing but peace and satisfaction with the world in which she lived. That's why Timbro was frustrated almost to the point of anger when these big thinking women came around filling his wife's head with nonsense about paints and stitchery and photographs and such. Wanted her to go down to the armory and stick her hands in the mud and make pots and pans and whatnot out of it, and pay good money for the privilege of doing so. He'd never heard of such a thing.

"You can pout all you want," he told her from his place at the head of the kitchen table where he awaited his dinner. "I'm just trying to save you some heartache is all I'm doing."

"I ain't pouting," Dobie answered, her face pink from the heat as she arranged her carrots and potatoes like flowers in bloom around the limp knot of roasted pork on the platter.

Timbro spread his hardened hands on the tablecloth before him, positioning his fingers just so around the spirals and curly-cues Dobie had embroidered on a piece of fabric she had rescued from his mother's attic. He had an obligation to protect his wife from frivolities, he reminded himself. Left to her own devices, there'd be no telling how she might spend both her time and his money.

Dobie smoothed the intricate braid at the back of her head then polished a smudge from a jelly jar before pouring Timbro a glass of sweet tea infused with mint from her garden. She carefully folded a cloth, quilted in shades of blue, into a perfect square and placed it in the middle of the kitchen counter to balance the yellow of a bowl full of apples, glossy and red. She pinched a sprig of larkspur from a pot in her kitchen window and placed it in the button hole of a corduroy dress she had cut down and sewn from one of Timbro's old brown suits, the lavender, stirring her eyes and causing them to dance as she approached the table, supper in hand.

Seating herself to his side, Dobie looked on as her husband served up the meal.

"Besides," Timbro told her, sniffing and shaking salt on his food before raising a fork. "Let's face it – you're a housewife. Creativity ain't got nothing to do with that."

Dobie looked out the window at the sun she noticed was setting like a ripe peach in a puddle of cranberry juice and nodded her head. Reaching for a potato, peeled and trimmed into a perfect sphere, she slowly began to hum.

Alvin and Alvie

For Alvie, the pain of losing her momma wasn't nearly so bad as the pain that her daddy still lived. This realization came to the girl like a bird falling out of the sky. Pretty summer day, clear blue sky full of possibilities and dreams set flying. Then, out of the blue, like a jaybird that once soared and pecked and played with its friends and then fell still and cold at the young girl's feet, feathers only ruffling in the breeze. Dead. Alive. And there it was. Alvie swatted at a family of gnats that buzzed around her sweet, wide face, sniffed hard, and nodded at the grass that needed cutting. The barn door was wide open now. She might as well go get the mower.

Alvin Tomler sat in the straight-backed chair that leaned into the sill of the bedroom window and watched his daughter's shape disappear inside the barn door. His eyes closed without will as she emerged, elbows bent, legs stretched long, pushing the leaden mower he should have replaced years ago. Good. The child's work lifted an unwanted burden from his back. Men's work. Alvin hated it.

Alvin Tomler hated women, too – that was news to no one. For years, people had just assumed that the man hated everybody. But after a while, the acts of kindness he

31

showed to his neighbors – Jim Taylor, Horace Watson, Monroe Potts, others – began to add up. A hand with a broken fence here, a ride into town there and, before long, Alvin Tomler was just another dirt farmer. One of the men. But the women of the community, they knew to steer clear of him. It wasn't just the looks he gave them that spoke not of the sexual danger their mothers had taught them to fear from men, but more to a kind of visceral disgust that seemed to bellow up from Alvin Tomler's stomach and make the ladies feel shame just for shopping on the same aisle in the market, or passing him on the road into town. Alvin's hatred reminded the women less of the way their husbands made them feel – weak, hungry – and more of the way the poorest girls, the overweight and ugly girls had made them feel in high school – guilty, unworthy, needing to apologize but unable to say for what.

Most had thought that once the baby was born, Alvin would soften up. And maybe that's what Alvie's momma had thought, too, when she held the newborn girl's face in her hands and looked into her eyes; the same mud-brown eyes as those of the boy who had one day without warning, knocked her roughly onto her belly on the gravel behind the Nehi sign, planted a child deep within her and never touched her again, save for a peck on the cheek when the preacher said he should. She named the girl "Alvie" and hoped for the best.

The little house where Alvie and her daddy now lived alone looked sad – like it missed her momma, too. The petunias needed dead-heading, the porch needed sweeping, the windows were muddy and streaked from spring rains. Alvie's momma had died on a cold March day in the middle of her kitchen floor. A dribble of blood trickled from her nose where the Formica had smacked her on the way down. The fire department came to the house just as the ambulance was leaving and removed a smoking pan of charred black biscuits that nobody had smelled burning in the oven. Three days later, her momma in the ground, Alvie went back to school and

Alvin moved from his recliner into the room where his wife had slept alone for seventeen years, and that's all there was to that.

Luckily, Alvie could step easily into her momma's kitchen shoes. Nothing more than a ghost in English and math classes, Alvie was a whiz at Home Economics. Against her daddy's approval, her momma had taken Alvie's blue ribbons from the county fair, pinned them to a piece of red felt, and tacked them, all in a row, over the girl's bed. Pies. Breads. Pickles and jellies. Alvie had a knack. And this day, the rows of shorn grass resembling dumplings laid straight in a deep-dish pan reminded her there was a good supper to look forward to putting on the stove after the work outside was done. Men's work. Alvie hated it.

The growl of the mower battered Alvin's windowpanes, dulling his ears. He watched as the girl's hips pushed strong behind her, their roundness moving like ball bearings, efficiently, provocatively, beautifully. Alvin rose from the chair and let his hands reach backwards to his own broad hips finding hard bone there where pliable tissue might have been. He gripped his hands into fists and swept his sight from the window to the walls to the floor.

Little had changed in his dead wife's room other than his presence there. His work shirts and overalls still hung separate from hers in a closet in the hall; his underwear, cleaned and folded, still materialized like magic in a drawer in the back room desk. Her things, photographs in frames, tatted doilies, a milky blue vase that had never held flowers, were positioned about the room purposefully and Alvin let them be. Though he had rarely ventured into the space when his wife lived, it took him little time to find comfort there after her death. The tired walls wore the same accumulation of dull white paint they'd worn when the newlyweds moved in, but the bedspread – pink chenille, he'd heard the woman say – softened the space as the dotted Swiss curtains fluttered like wings in the wind. He cried, the first night he slept in the bed. Not for its emptiness, nor for the lack of the woman who was gone, but for the vast softness of the sheets, the sunshine fragrance they emitted and the way his body, fully clothed and frightened, felt the touch of the fabric. Felt the caress. Softness. When the sun woke him the next morning, his face flushed and his head swam. He touched nothing in the room but returned to the bed every night from then on.

Outside the window, Alvie shoved the machine over toadstools and anthills and occasional bare spots in the yard where grass never grew. The bib to her overalls weighed against her breasts and the heavy leather boots rubbed at her ankles, but her contempt of the clothes her daddy made her wear had become such a part of the girl that she barely knew it was there. It mattered little when she was younger – the denim and flannel were comfortable for play despite the teasing that came from other little girls whose mothers' dressed them in lace and bows. But as her body and awareness grew, she found herself caught up in envy of the fullness and well-placed lines the other girls so proudly put on display. It was something her momma could see and, one day, in a frustrated fit of maternal rebellion, she made up her mind that under-cover at least, something had to change. From then on, pretty things began to appear, literally, under the covers of Alvie's bed. Pastel panties with lace; bras with tiny pink bows in the front; sanitary napkins; scented talc. Now, with her momma gone, Alvie wore these treasures close to her skin and her heart, quietly aware of the sweetness of her momma's touch, even beneath the coarseness of the clothes her daddy no longer had to insist she wear. And on days like today when the sun bore down and the jagged shards of grass scratched at her ankles and knees, she found herself reaching often into the neck of her shirt to stroke the bit of satin she had secreted there.

Having become absorbed, as he often did, in the textures and colors of the dead woman's room, Alvin noticed neither his daughter's discomfort nor the completion of her outdoor chores. The room felt both perfect and foreign, like a place where he could visit but never stay, as he found himself visually rummaging through the surroundings, searching for his bearings. He placed his palm against the wall and let his fingertips trail along the plaster as if feeling for a pulse – window to corner to closet door which, ajar as it had been since his daughter had chosen the clothes in which to bury her mother, seemed to beckon to him with fabrics and patterns and scents. He peered inside. The woman's clothes still hung there. Calico housedresses, frayed sweaters, dark dresses for church. He leaned into the smell, a muted mixture of lavender, cleanness and dough and, quivering, reached in his calloused hand and, just for a moment, let it be.

In the front of the house, the screened door slammed and he jerked his hand away, as if from a flame. His own pulse raced and he retreated to the bed, the only spot in the room where he felt passably at home. He sat on the edge and inhaled the teases that sneaked in from the kitchen.

Grease and black pepper – fried chicken. Fat back, vinegar, heavy salt – greens. He hung his head as the gnawing in his stomach reached up to his mouth and brought water.

Then he saw them, on the floor under a heavy layer of dust, barely peeking out from the curtain of pom-poms that trimmed the chenille spread on the bed. Shoes. Soft black leather, a small squat heel, perfect lace rosette perched on a shiny toe. Church shoes. The motion to touch them came without intention, and he pulled a single shoe to his lap and sat it on his knee like an old man might hold a child. Tentatively, he let the fingers of one hand slide into the toe of the shoe and spread out so that his knuckles grazed the felted lining and his fingertips patted the quilted inner sole.

Bacon grease sizzled in a cast iron pan as tomatoes, sliced green from the vine and dredged in cornmeal and egg, hissed and spat.

Alvin let his mind drift through hunger and sensation to a different time, a different place, but still, shoes. He could smell a similar supper cooking in the kitchen; could hear summer birds out the window in the trees; could feel the wonder of the fabric in the shoe, not on his hand but on his own small foot, pockmarked with blisters and bug bites and the grime from a day played hard. He felt himself moving into that place hidden in his soul where a neglected memory dwelled. He knew the place; knew the rambling path to get there; knew the thickets and briars that had concealed the opening for years and warned him when to look away lest the feeling return.

Sliced apple, Crisco, cinnamon – pie with flaky crust. It took him in and away.

The shoes engulfed his little-boy feet, allowing his tiny toes plenty of room to curl and wiggle and stretch. He stood tall but awkwardly in them and scuffed forward, a veiled black hat, prim and proper, balanced on his bobbing head; a rope of pearly beads strung round his neck. The lipstick he had fished from his mother's purse, that was swaying at a crook in his arm, felt waxy on his face and barely disguised the stain of juice on his lips, but he liked the feel of it. Most importantly, as he surveyed his reflection in the mirror on his parents' wall, he liked the look of it – the look of himself.

"I'm beautiful," he whispered to the room he thought empty and safe.

Then, a gasp. He had never felt the kind of pain that walloped him on the side of his head, sending him sprawling across the floor, the net from the hat scraping a raw place on his cheek – not even when he fell from the top of the church steps and landed, broken armed and bloody-lipped, on the sidewalk below. Even now, grown-man Alvin could taste the salt of the blood that had filled his little-boy mouth; could see the huge white flesh of the back of his father's hand as it rose and struck again and again. Grown man Alvin grabbed his side and winced, once again absorbing the impact of steel-toed boot on tender, growing ribs. He had long ago lost the words his father gave him on that day, but the message was dull-knife carved into his chest: Bad. Worse than bad – wrong. Worse than wrong – abominable.

In the kitchen, Alvie rubbed at the thin skin of a Vidalia onion, balanced it on its side and, grasping her momma's sharpest knife, began to slice layer after layer of juicy intertwined rings. The sweet acid smell of the onion had little effect on the young girl's eyes but, as it wafted down the hall and into the bedroom, it intensified and overtook her father's head. He squeezed his face into a tight and wrinkled mass but the hot burn at the back of his nose and eyes met the searing pain in his gut and coalesced into a wound as raw as the day it was delivered. The tears came like a hemorrhage, washing the man's face and body and pulling him to the floor on his knees where he found himself in a place he hadn't been in such a long time – inside himself. Wrapping his arms across his chest, hard muscles pulsing in each palm, he curled like a baby on the soft hooked rug, a splay of cabbage roses and curly-cues and ferns, and let his tears pour into the loops of wool.

The gurgle of hot coffee perking on the stove pulled open his eyes and brought him slowly to his feet; his stomach pointing him toward the kitchen. Alvie noticed something different about her daddy's eyes as soon as he walked in the room – a sleepy, drunken look that caught hers time and again throughout the meal. There were moments when she thought he might smile. The painful quiet that usually accompanied their meals was oddly interspersed with little sounds from her daddy that, had she not known better, seemed to indicate something like pleasure, almost delight. The man who had gulped down his breakfast never lifting his eyes from his plate, was actually tasting his supper and scanning the room, letting his gaze rest on sights he'd never seemed to see – a pile of polished red apples in a bright yellow bowl; faded dish towels, folded and ready for the drawer; a seersucker apron, blue and dusted with flour, that his daughter had removed just before sitting at the table.

Pushing her chair back, Alvie rose to clear the table, reaching for an empty chicken platter when her daddy also took it in his hand. They stood, facing one another and all the space and time and ache between them. Alvin cleared his throat and closed his eyes as he spoke, "Let me," he said. "Let me."

Raylene

The idea that anything Lula said could be something other than a hoot had never crossed Raylene's mind. She loved going to the little mill village beauty shop for the banter and the foolishness as much as she did for the attention Lula gave to the top of her head. She had tried to convince herself that the conceit of an occasional shampoo and set was something she did more for her husband than for herself. But when Dewey got the call from the Lord to become the associate pastor of the Church of the Beloved Body of Christ the same week that a Saturday morning slot opened miraculously at Lula's shop, Raylene was convinced it was the Lord's will her hair be pretty. So she booked herself in perpetuity. In some ways she did it for Dewey; in others, she did it for the Lord.

Lula had a knack for working people into a lather, both literally and figuratively. She would read a story about a half alien baby in *The National Enquirer*, or see a segment on *60 Minutes* about a campground full of nudists, then relay a portion of the information she had learned to the women in her shop, embellishing the parts she could not recall. Raylene would hear snippets of Lula's latest broadcast in line at the Winn Dixie, or catch a familiar phrase before the chatter died down in Sunday school, and know what was on everybody's mind. Always on her best behavior, Raylene rarely took part in any discourse that teetered near the theatric. Even as a grown woman, there was enough little lady in her to know when to best look at her feet and smile.

But on the rare morning when business at the shop was slow, or if Lula wasn't feeling hoarse from a hard week's work, she would occasionally engage Raylene as her private audience. No stranger to the shortfalls of humanity, Lula could be counted on to apply pristine judgment to the workings of the world. It was with this prudence that she introduced Raylene to the concept of the *women's libber*.

"Right there in the road with both Bert Parks and God looking on," Lula rasped, her voice hardly a whisper but the certainty of scandal in her eyes. "Hairspray, curlers, make-up, what have you, right into a fifty-five gallon drum. Some even threw in their bras and girdles, if you can believe that! Stripped 'em right off their bodies, tossed 'em in, and – *whoosh!* Up in flames!"

It wasn't that Raylene was insensitive to Lula's distress at the destruction of articles of beauty. In fact, the very idea of throwing away a perfectly good lipstick made her gasp. But the thought of summarily dispensing with a bra struck a tender nerve somewhere near her breastbone and she felt herself squirm beneath her own elastic, lace, and wire.

The kind of woman who wore her brassier like a second layer of skin, the concept of not wearing it was as foreign to Raylene as going barefoot in the rain or dancing in the street. She wore her bra like she wore her own smell. The only thing she took off her body less than her bra was her wedding band, and only then because it needn't be laundered or changed. Raylene wore her bra to shop in, to clean in, and to sleep in. It was the last thing she took off before bathing and the first thing she put back on. It wasn't that she wanted to wear it, or that she even liked wearing it. She had made no conscious decision in the matter. She wore her bra because that was what women did, which was all she thought she needed to know.

Raylene left Lula's shop that Saturday morning with an uneasy feeling swimming about her head. Try as she might she couldn't shake Lula's story and, throughout her walk home, she revisited the idea with a guilty sense of confusion. Never one to notice her own body, much less that of another woman, Raylene began to let her eyes slide down the faces of the women she encountered to the area below their chins and, finally, to their breasts. Aware that God could read her every thought she quickly reassured both Him, and herself, that she had no untoward interests in the women; their brassieres were where her interests lie.

But once the day's duties were done and she found herself alone in the little tile bathroom where she freshened and changed her clothes before Dewey came home for supper, her own image in the mirror caught her eye. Raylene couldn't remember the last time she had looked at her body; it was as much a stranger to her as it was to Dewey, who sought only specific parts and then in the quiet ambiguity of the dark. The woman in the mirror wore white cotton panties below a sturdy brassiere that crossed her heart neatly, leaving a narrow ribbon of flesh in between.

Eyes closed, Raylene slid the fingers of one hand down her neck, across her shoulder and under the strap. The cool touch of her hand gave way to a deep and glowing warmth. She took a breath and let her palm move further down, across skin that felt sumptuous – like a velveteen coat. There was a roundness below she could sense as much as feel – a whole, satisfying, centering roundness that took Raylene's thoughts out of the bathroom and into her summer garden where she cupped her palm around the imperfect sphere of a ripe tomato, full and warmed by morning sun. It took her into the sweet smells of her morning kitchen, where a raised mound of dough was firm, living, ready to reinvent itself as hot buttered biscuits. It took her to the furry belly of a childhood pup – round and wonderful and sated with absolute trust.

41

The grind of gravel in the driveway told her that Dewey was home from the church. Out the window she could see the splat of fresh spring rain dot the windshield of his car. His keys jingled in the back door then, *slam*, and all the air in the house pushed through the doorways and walls.

"I'm home," he called as he sifted the mail in his hands. He could hear the pat of Raylene's feet down the hallway and through the kitchen, then away toward the back porch and door. He looked up into the emptiness of the kitchen and realized she had come and gone.

The rain, no longer a drizzle, ran in sleek rivulets down the window panes that looked out Raylene's kitchen onto the street and the houses and shops and churches beyond.

"Raylene?" Dewey called, wiping the fog from the window. "Good God, Raylene, where are you?"

And in the middle of the tar and gravel road that took the woman everywhere she went in the world in which she lived, Raylene stood, feet bare, face raised to heaven, arms extended like a wind mill in the steady rain that streamed and puddled in a tender valley between her breasts, separated from the world by nothing more than a thin layer of cotton and the unmistakable veil of joy.

Thomas

The dogs howled the night that Daddy died – a chordless, melodic song that, from far away, might have sounded like wind that had lost its way. But from my bedroom window sounded of nothing but heartache, humiliation, and the blunt-headed sadness that he would be there no more. I felt it, too. If I could, I would have hollered right along with them, finding that low moan from deep in my throat, that acid taste that rises up from an aching belly. The magnetic core of all my family's pain and joy had spun off and away, into the night, leaving behind a singular hum that even broken old dogs could pick up and sing along to. A heel to the haunch; a fist to the face – the bittersweet sting that he knew we were alive.

I hurt most for Momma. Even as a boy I knew she had built her life around him. The sun rose and set by the biscuits she made for Daddy's meals. They came with country ham and red eye gravy in the morning and pinto beans with chow-chow at night. In between the cooking and chopping and frying, Momma would *do up* Daddy's shirts, as she called it, washing them in the machine he'd bought for her birthday the year I turned three. It was a cast enameled prize – bought on time – that validated her position among the other women of the county and he placed it conspicuously on the front porch of our house for the entire world to see. Momma grimaced every time we drove up in the yard and she

saw it there, bottom and sides rusty from rain and angry dog
pee; electrical cord stretched, like a silly leash, along the wall,
over the sill, and into a hole Daddy had poked in the front
window screen with a cottonwood switch.

She washed his work clothes in that machine with
soap from the same laundry powder box that produced our
Sunday drinking glasses, carefully collected throughout the
years of my childhood, protected and polished and placed on
a high shelf far away from clumsy little hands. She shelled
beans for his table and burned fat for his gravy. She cut his
hair and scrubbed his sink and swept the dust from his boots
with an old flour sack. She made his bed and bore his babies. He was her day and night and I worried about her the
night that he died as I lay in my bed and listened to the howl
of dogs that would never be beaten again. Just as they had
traded their physical pain for an aching spirit, I knew that my
Momma would wake up soon to a morning full of wondering.

They had married on a rainy July morning, standing
before the justice of the peace in clothes store-bought special for the occasion with money that might better have put
curtains on the windows or cans in the cupboard. But Daddy
was proud and Momma was quiet, so they went wanting into
the first long months of their lives together. I came that December, too soon for the church or propriety, and announced
myself with relentless colic that wore my Daddy's nerves to
a nub. Momma couldn't keep me quiet and the house got
too small for both Daddy and my cries so he took to sleeping
cramped and restless nights in the cab of his pick-up truck
parked in the yard beneath a pawpaw tree. The good job he
had at the mill was lost to tardiness and a general disaffec-
tion for his attitude, the Boss Man determining that Daddy's
shoulder was heavy with the weight of lost hopes, lost opportunities, and lost time, thusly adding to his empty hands and
pockets with another lost situation.

Work was scarce then, which temporarily drove Momma into Mr. Henry's cotton fields, with me in a sling on her back or hanging from her shoulder like ripe fruit on a vine. Daddy took what jobs he could find, often unbeknownst to him until the back of the truck he rode in delivered him to a site where he was handed a hoe or a pick or a shovel. Occasional Saturdays would find Momma in line in the church parking lot, hands out and filled with a brown paper bag of the odd canned goods the congregation gathered for people like us. For the needy. On those days, Daddy's hand could also be found wrapped around a brown paper bag, his emitting a tangy, sweet odor that replicated itself on his breath until night fell, and he drifted off to sleep on the sofa with the radio playing Jimmy Dean or Patsy Cline.

Other nights knew no such peace.

Daddy never used his fists on Momma, hitting her instead with an open hand like he would a bad child; upon her back, her head and thighs. The hand that reared up high in the air would fall down onto her as if of its own accord, time and time again, Momma drawing her head into her chest like a learned boxer, until finally the hand would quiver in the air and, eyes closed, he would bring it down, red, and shake away the pain and the blood that pulsed in his fingertips. The screened door would slam against the front porch wall then ricochet back and close softly within its frame. The aspirin bottle smelled of vinegar as Momma poured uncounted tablets into her hand and washed them down with cold well water then wiped her face with a clean dish rag. On those nights, we tucked ourselves into bed.

But there were sweet nights, too. Nights of slow dances to tunes hummed into quietness, feet planted but bodies swaying, Daddy's chin laid soft on top of Momma's head; me and the girls tip-toeing to bed. Nights of us chasing fireflies and playing shadow tag in dewy grass way past bedtime while they laughed on the porch, shared beer from a bottle, whispering until he slept, his head in her lap. Nights of piggyback rides in clean pajamas, prayers spoken to the song of crickets through the window while he listened, head-bowed, at the bedroom door.

It was the sweet nights I hated most. Unlike the mean nights of swearing and drinking, the sweet nights saved and seduced and ravaged my Momma. Their promises left her bruised, if not beaten, and bore her a crop of disappointment she could gather into a basket like wild summer plums, crusty with syrup and full of worms. The sweet nights came in spells, lasting days or weeks, giving her due cause for hopes and plans. "This time," she'd think. "Maybe this time ...."

It had been a season of sweet nights, that November day when Daddy was to die. Hunting had been good and there was rabbit in the freezer. Christmas was approaching – not soon, really – but close enough to bring goose pimples to our boney little arms and a tiny dance in Momma's eyes when she mentioned Santa Claus' peeping. The smell of sweet potatoes bathed in shortening and baking in the oven filled the house, while beans bubbled on the stove and Momma sang a tune I didn't know.

When the door slammed shut it woke the baby and set her to crying. Always afraid of storms, she had mistaken the bang for thunder, and experience had taught us to best just hold her in our arms until her tears subsided. But Daddy was already raw. His words were a whisper but they were drenched in whiskey and came out with spit and fumes and fire. "Shut her up," he grumbled, bending to unlace a mud-caked boot. Her arms reached up as she toddled toward me and I scooped her up by her bottom and began the pacing and jostling that should ultimately quieten her down.

Daddy sank into the couch, sighed hard and lit a cigarette, then closed his eyes. With his left hand he rubbed at his face and his forehead and finally the entirety of his head, squeezing fingertips into his skull as if it were a rubber ball he could fling far away, off toward the horizon. Smoke lay in the air, muddling the smell of supper and the baby continued to cry.

"I said, shut her up," he growled at me, still quiet, but teeth bared, eyes squinted against the light.

The baby's long legs knocked into my knees as I held on with both arms, bouncing her against my chest, trying to stifle her cries with my shoulder.

"I'm trying, Daddy," I said through jaws clinched tight, sweat running cold down the back of my shirt.

I caught myself and inhaled fast, trying to suck the very words that had escaped my mind back into my throat. I knew not to say anything to Daddy. I'd learned that a long time ago and knew it then, even as the words were coming out of my mouth, even as the ashtray soared past my head and shattered like a bottle rocket against the living room wall. I winced and waited, and for a moment there were no sounds at all – even the baby had gone quiet, her face buried in my shoulder, her arms and legs squeezing so tight as to crawl up my body, to the top of my head and away from it all.

Then, it came.

"Trying!" he bellowed at me, his voice now that of an ancient monster, a loosed bear, a rabid dog with no con- science, no intent other than harm. He was on his feet now, unsteady but making progress across the floor toward us. "You're trying?" he cried again, demanding an answer I didn't have.

Maybe it was instinct; maybe I'd seen Momma do it so many times before that I just knew what to do without think- ing. I found myself crouched in the corner, the baby folded into a ball between my chest and the wall; my head low, my slight back a puny but resolute shield for us both. I tensed myself into a stone and waited for the fall.

But there were footsteps from the kitchen and it was Momma that yanked me up by my arm and told me to run to Mr. Henry's place; told me to take the girls and go. *Just go.* She stood straight and tight, her feet planted squarely on the floor, and she held an opened beer in her outstretched hand toward my Daddy and, trembling, turned her head toward

47

the side, braced her quivering chin against her shoulder, and waited for him to strike.

Holding my little sister's hand and in the perfect illumination of that fresh winter's day, the air crisp and alive and tingly, I moved west toward the Henry place, hitching the baby up higher on my hip with every few steps I took. The sun was just high enough overhead to throw stringy shadows into the woods and we looked like long thin giants running across the field.

Mrs. Henry sat us down at her freshly wiped kitchen table while she put chunks of buttered cornbread into big clay mugs and filled them with cold milk from the icebox. We shoveled the mush into our mouths with heavy tablespoons we could hardly handle, letting the grainy texture of the bread soften on our tongues then slide down our throats while the butter rose to the top of the milk in oily golden clouds.

At first, the scream of the siren came from way off, like the whine of a cicada far away. We were sitting at Mrs. Henry's table drawing pictures of scarecrows onto brown paper bags with fat crayon nubs we'd fished out of the Henry grandchildren's coffee can full of worn pencils and stubs of colors and chalk.

In the country, sound carries. Freight trains can pass and be heard ten miles away. Even our young ears were trained to detect the location of a siren, its speed and its direction – usually heading toward the pool hall where frustrated men took out their rage on angry boys drunk and desperate enough to rile the wrong man for very little reason at all. Sometimes the wail came near, pausing, then whirring once again before it faded as it sped frantically toward the county hospital and out of our ear's range.

That evening the scream started quietly, as a moan, and grew louder and stronger while we colored and kept our eyes on our papers, until it approached the mailbox at the end of the long Henry drive, and passed. I looked up and out the back window just as the sun was setting beyond the cotton field, sending fingers the color of Christmas oranges out over the tops of the pines at the field's edge. Swaths of blue and violet and pink hovered above the trees like angels. I finally let myself think and the truth grabbed my shoulders like a strong man. Hollering to the girls, I picked the baby up by the waist and ran out the Henry kitchen door, Mrs. Henry behind us, wiping dishwater from her hands on the skirt of her dress. Ignoring the path, I wrestled the baby higher onto my hip and cut through the brambles, jumping the ditches and letting the briars dig into my tender shins.

Our house looked like a skull as we approached it, the windows glowing like eye sockets, the front door a gaping mouth emitting a sallow yellow light that spilled out of it and onto our patchy front yard. Strangers were about, inside and out, and the door screeched painfully as I opened the screen and went inside. The house smelled of vomit.

Momma sat on her heels, as if in prayer, in the middle of the living room floor. Streaks of tears and snot dripped from her chin as she wiped at the floor with an old dish rag. I only saw Daddy's face for a second before they covered him with a sheet, pure white and starched stiff, then wheeled him out through the kitchen and into the back of the ambulance that was parked by his truck in our yard.

"Wasn't anything I could've done," she said, looking past me and the girls and the rescue men, "even if I'd a wanted."

The Henry's finally left and Momma had us tuck ourselves into bed that night, so I wiped the girls' noses and listened to their prayers, and pecked each one of them on the cheek before they went to sleep. I could smell the bleach she was using to wash the floor as it wafted down the hall, into my room, and out my bedroom window toward the back of the house where the dogs howled, already in mourning. I drifted off in a sweaty worry and was surprised when the day dawned bright.

It took me a minute to rearrange my thoughts the

next morning and remember how life had changed in an instant the night before. I lay still in my bed and listened to the familiar chug of the washing machine on the porch and the reassuring sizzle of a fire in the kitchen stove. Something was missing from my morning smells though and I skated my bare feet along the cold wooden floor into the kitchen where Momma and the girls were already up and dressed. On the table were bowls of steaming oatmeal and plates of cinnamon toast, scrambled eggs speckled with pepper, strips of bacon fried just right, hotcakes and a jar of molasses steeping in a pot of hot water, but not a biscuit in sight.

"Good morning, Thomas," Momma sang, rising from a new place at the table then bending down to kiss the top of my head. "Breakfast is ready," and she gestured to the table with a flourish. "Help yourself."

Uncle Flu

It had fallen upon the nephews to pack up and clean out Uncle Flu's room at the nursing home and, though I didn't expect anyone else to show up, I rose with the birds and headed down the highway to Camden on the designated Saturday in May. The drive from Greenville was into the sun and I chased a headache with strong coffee and a BC Powder. That was one of the tricks Uncle Flu had taught me. "Never let a pain get a hold a' you," he used to say, gripping a hand-ful of demon-filled air with his fist. "Get a hold a' that pain first!" Then he would cast the angry notion away with an open palm to the wind. The image of pain as an object or a creature a body could catch and hold within their hand, then dispense with at will, has stayed with me my entire life.

The second son to John Thomas Douglas, Uncle Flu was given the name Fluellen because when Grandpa John was in the First World War, he had his first and only experience with live theater. And it made him cry. Twice. It was in Dover, and members of an enthusiastic Shakespearean troupe out of London had come down to entertain the soldiers before they enjoined the battle on the continent. Given the impending situation and the intimacy the soldiers would soon have with war, the actors chose the play *Henry V* to perform for the men. According to the story told too many times by Grandpa John, the play made him cry the only two times he had ever cried in his life. The first was for the pride that he felt, like the noble Prince Hal on Saint Crispin's Day, at being one of the "few," the "happy few," the "band of brothers" who would soon lay their lives on the line for the sake of war and honor. The second tears were shed from his laughing so hard when Captain Fluellen, the waggish Welshman in the play, forced the soldier Pistol to eat the leek that Fluellen wore proudly in his cap in honor of St. Davy's Day. "If you can mock a leek you can eat a leek," Grandpa John used to mimic, then sigh and say, "I laughed until I cried."

So my grandfather held onto the name Fluellen and, after his first son was born who, by all rights would be named as his junior, his second boy got the name Fluellen, and Grandpa John had a fine and impressive story to tell for the rest of his life.

But there was more to the naming of the boys than stories. Grandpa John had plans. The greatest failure of his life was the battle that fate had not allowed him to fight. Shortly after his brush with Shakespeare, Grandpa John slipped on a splattered potato in the mess tent and fell to an unforgiving concrete floor, striking his back on a stainless steel serving table's edge and shattering bones and damaging nerves in his right shoulder and arm. He was sent home with little to no fanfare in a cast and a sling on the same day the rest of his company were sent into the muddy and bloody trenches of France. Unable to fulfill the rightful destiny of a soldier, Grandpa John determined that he would sire boys with no greater goal in life than battle. The third and fourth children of my grandparents, my mother and my Aunt Grace, were so inconsequential to Grandpa John that he told my grandmother that if she could do no better than to bring forth females, they might as well quit trying. Which they did.

My headache nearly gone, I veered off the highway that had tracked through the sand hills of South Carolina and onto a magnolia lined avenue which would lead me to the last home Uncle Flu ever knew; a convalescent refuge for life and battle weary old military men who had nowhere else to go and nothing else to do, but wait, remember, and die. Dozens of American flags, flown in honor of Memorial Day, popped and cracked in the wind. The saddest irony was that, for Uncle Flu, those last years spent in the company of other old men were likely some of the least lonely days of his life.

Uncle Flu never married. But the story was told of a love he left in France when stationed near the rolling pastures of Bayeux after Normandy. My mother and Aunt Grace never knew the details and weren't even sure how much of the tale was factual and how much they themselves had added and embellished throughout the intervening years. But it was common lore among the Douglas clan that Uncle Fluellen had either left or lost a love he had once, in some off handed and unintentional way, referred to as his "Jewel" in France.

The sisters would stand in the windows of bustling kitchens and messy dining rooms during family gatherings and watch Uncle Flu as he hoisted his nephews on his shoulders and blew pristine dandelion seeds with his nieces on hot summer days. They would "tsk, tsk" the loneliness of his life and bemoan the family of his own Flu never got to enjoy. Time and again they plied their match making skills, setting Flu up with bosomy classmates, young business-suited career women, then widows from their church who smelled of lavender and cinnamon, all of whom Flu treated to chivalric evenings of crisp Chablis, kindness, and etiquette, and never called again.

Instead, Fluellen was like a second father to us all. A constant and abiding presence in the lives of the cousins, Flu never missed an opportunity to show his support for his nieces and nephews. If there was a dance recital or a Little League game, Flu was there. Marching band half-time shows, sidewalk art exhibits, and science fairs filled his social calendar. It didn't matter what kind of vegetable, celestial being, or forest creature our grammar school play directors made us dress up as, Uncle Flu led our cheering section from front row center.

Flu was there for us behind the scenes as well. When David, Aunt Grace's husband, died early and out of the blue from a heart attack, leaving Grace with three boys to raise on her own and a house payment that she and David could just barely make when he was alive, it was Uncle Flu who stepped in. Somehow, Grace paid her house off early and those boys learned not only how to launder a load of clothes, all the way down to starching collars, but also how to change the oil in a car and replace a drain pipe under the kitchen sink. And when the reputation of Grace's oldest boy, Davie, started winding about town and made its way across the counter of the hardware store Uncle Flu managed, it was Flu who not only set Davie down for a talking-to, but accompanied the boy to the local pharmacy and taught him a few of the more embarrassing parts of what being a man is all about.

The white brick entrance to the nursing home approached and I slowed to turn into the drive and inspect the flag that Uncle Flu had taken his turn among the more able old men in raising over the past few years. When one of the cousins came to visit, Flu would purposefully raise the standard so that it was upside down with stars pointing at dirt and stripes waving toward heaven. "I'm just an old man," he'd whine pitifully to the nursing attendants, who chastised him but seldom corrected the error. Then he'd snicker, nudge us in the ribs with a quick and boney elbow, wink hard, and sometimes try to tousle our hair with his spotted but still strong hands. Uncle Flu loved a good joke - especially when the person it was on never had a clue.

I pulled into an empty parking space and was surprised to find, already parked, the cars of two of Aunt Grace's sons, Henry and Tom. I stood alongside our cars for a moment, stretched my legs and surveyed the last place Uncle Flu called home. A series of low roofed buildings made of red brick painted white, windows painted permanently shut, stood bright and gleaming between small knolls of new spring green. Bluebird houses cleaved to the trunks of pecan trees across an expansive lawn, and a fine garden of azaleas, some still clinging to their bloom, lined the path that led toward the nursing home entrance. I could pick out Flu's old room, one ... two ... three windows up from the emergency exit at the end of the building. Tom waved to me from inside and I threw up my hand and hurried in to greet the cousins I hadn't seen since the funeral.

While Flu had occupied an important and often visited corner of all of our lives as we were growing up, it was the wife, sons, and daughters of Uncle John, Jr., whose worlds were frequently set back in balance by Flu's deft hand. Some people say it was Grandpa John who put so much pressure on his first born that there was no way the son could live up to the expectations of the father. Some say that John, Jr. was not so much lacking the mettle of the warrior his father had hoped he'd be, as he was lacking the moral fortitude of someone dedicated enough to do the right thing when he was supposed to, and not do the wrong thing when he wasn't. For this, Grandpa John and the fairly expandable if not limitless boundaries he had given to his son were not without blame. For whatever reason, the first born son of John Thomas Douglas had barely embraced manhood when he promptly brought shame on the family name.

It was before either my sisters or I were born - Flu, my mother, and Grace were still small children themselves - but lips loosened by too much Christmas wine and sisterly whispers on back porch steps provided the cousins and myself with enough bits and pieces of the story to know that a very young girl, what by today's standards would be considered criminal conduct, and a dishonorable discharge from the United States Army, dated November 22, 1941, were central to the plot.

What we know more about is what happened after the disgrace.

Having volunteered for the armed forces immediately after graduation, and just before signing the license to marry his high school sweetheart, both John and his father had felt secure that all the pieces to a Medal of Honor puzzle were coming together as they had planned. John Jr.'s celibacy, enforced by his father throughout high school, was soon, as promised, properly rewarded by a pretty young wife, ripe and ready for maternity. The seed happily sown, the eager patriot boarded a bus which would take him first to boot camp, then away beyond purple mountains' majesty and onto the field of battle.

It has always been worth questioning what caused father and son the greater of the distresses that would follow John, Jr.'s enlistment in the army. Was it the unthinkable transformation of the much anticipated battle field into the sandy shores of the Hawaiian Islands and the concomitant frustration at the lack of a true call to arms? Or was it the government's unwillingness to bend to my grandfather's meticulously designed Douglas plan, a decision which would ultimately cost Uncle John the highly valued death he felt he deserved to give to his country? Whatever the answer, the stress and strain that so embraced my Uncle John, Jr. while he was not doing battle in Hawaii, complicated by an empty bed where, having waited so long and so patiently, he thought his wife rightly should have been, drove the young man to seek solace in the arms of far too many willing females and, at least one not so willing and, in fact, not even above the age of consent, had that been an option, as the story goes.

Uncle John, Jr. came home, disgraced, with a chip on his shoulder the size of Alabama, the inability to look his father in his steely blue eye, and a hell bent determination to make the District of Columbia and each and every occupant of a desk at the Pentagon pay emotional restitution for the lack of judgment he himself had exhibited during his call to duty. It was a convoluted and ironic case of shell shock that required John, Jr. to persecute government employees with threatening letters and the worst possible vulgarities of verbal harassment, as he asserted his claim that, rather than he, it was his service-induced deprivation from the matrimonial bed which was directly responsible for the violence of his actions, as well as the consequential illegitimate son that he left behind in a little shack outside of Pearl Harbor. Upon returning home to a wife, properly persuaded to stay put by a father-in-law adamant on the issue of his son's innocence and victimization, Uncle John began a slow descent into an emotional predicament which would neither allow him to face the dishonor of his actions nor let him forget that a wrong had been done.

The radio report that demanded the attention of every American on December 7, 1941, exactly two weeks to the day after John had packed his duffle and boarded a United States transport plane that swept him shamefully away from his place in infamy, proved to be the final fan to the inferno that would engulf Uncle John's sanity. He immersed himself in the search for a scapegoat and, to prove himself a man who knew some right from wrong, undertook a mission to make as many legitimate babies as his wife could accommodate. But, after more than two years of sleepless nights, nagging anger and, still, the inability to look his father in the eye, Uncle John, Jr. finally fought the only battle he had ever truly been allowed to fight and, in the end, both lost and won when he discharged a bullet into his forehead from the service revolver Grandpa John had given him for his fifteenth birthday.

Grandpa John managed to have his first born son's casket draped in a flag. He called on a few of his buddies from the VFW to solemnly present the trophy to the pregnant, but strangely at peace, widow on a rainy morning in August, just before Uncle Fluellen was to return for his final high school year. Flu left the funeral and spent the next few days mourning the loss of a brother and the waste of a soul, and avoiding the heavy hand of his father which eventually made its way to his shoulder, serving notice to any hopes Flu had held for completing his education.

It wasn't so much the demands of my grandfather that prompted Flu to pick up the torch of manhood that both his brother and his father had managed to drop. It was more his pity at the desperation his father had divulged, and the weight of the fact that he, Fluellen, the last of John Douglas's sons, was the sole person invested with the challenge of restoring the integrity of his own father's sense of worth. It was a grievous responsibility. But Flu took it up.

Uncle Flu spent the last few days before he signed up and shipped out making arrangements for school books and procuring supplies and rations for thick soled shoes for his fatherless nephews. He introduced his widowed sister-in-law to reading and bought her a stack of books which included Mortimer Adler's *How to Read a Book* and *The Autobiography of Alice B. Toklas*. For himself, he chose a collection of twenty-five of Dylan Thomas's poems and Richard Wright's *Native Son*, which he packed in his modest bag of belongings. Within a year, Fluellen found himself crammed into the hull of a rocking and lurching landing craft, back to back with forty-five other boys between the ages of seventeen and twenty-two, seasick, cramped and terrified, and crossing the English Channel to reclaim Cherbourg from the enemy's hands.

He lived through D-Day, and he lived through the rest of the war, but the remainder of Uncle Flu's military experiences in England and France are a mystery. While we know that he wore home a uniform displaying an assortment of ribbons, decorations and honors, we don't know on what grounds he was awarded them or what they all meant. Flu never would say. We also know that our uncle did not immediately return home when his enlistment was up. He spent more than a year in Brittany and Normandy, with occasional forays into Paris, and would likely be there still were it not for the anxious cables he received from Grandpa John pleading that he return home for his hero's due welcome. It was when Grandpa finally threatened to journey to France himself that Flu relented and ultimately returned to the States.

His uniform was wrinkled, giving the impression of it having spent more time than not forgotten in the bottom of a bag; his face thin, but not unhealthy; and his eyes swollen,

red, and distant when the family turned out to meet Flu on a
damp and foggy morning at the bus station in town. Despite
his father's enthusiasm, which included the first big, magnani-
mous hug and honest-to-God kiss on his face that the son
could ever remember receiving from his father, the sisters
knew that their brother was less than happy to be home. He
approached the family home place the way a man with a grave
toothache draws near the office of a dentist. His mother, who
had stayed in her kitchen so as to ensure warm bacon and
eggs immediately upon his arrival, remarked on the disorien-
tated hang of his clothes and the look on his face less like a
returning warrior and more like a little boy lost. It ended up
taking several months for Flu to slowly revert back to some
semblance of the young southern man he was before he
went to war. He was still gentle and attentive, and his books
became more of a refuge than ever. But it is said that it was
during those first few delicate months after his return that Flu
became the loneliest man around.

It was some twenty years later after the last prayers of
my Grandpa John's funeral that I heard my mother recall to
Flu how much the war had changed him. But Fluellen smiled
an odd little smile, and looked off over a break of white pine
trees at the edge of the cemetery and into the sky to a place
further away than any of us could ever travel and said, "No,
the war didn't change me. It simply made me more of who I
really am."

Tom had removed most of the items from the walls
and stacked them in a cardboard box by the wide, wheelchair
accessible door, and was sifting through the contents of the
closet. The room, once as cluttered and campy as a mill house
kitchen, already looked bare. After handshakes and hugs,
Tom recommended that I take a look through the three deep
drawers in the bureau that held the last belongings of Uncle
Flu's life. An English professor at the College of Charleston,
Henry had meticulously boxed up most of Flu's books to di-
vide later between the family members and was in the process

of making several trips with them to his car.

I grabbed an old orange crate and began emptying the contents of the drawers. A few pairs of pajamas, a week's worth of white undershirts and boxers, some sweaters and old-man-baggy pants. From the top drawer down, there was little spectacular about Flu's possessions. In the middle drawer I found bundles of notes and letters from the cousins when we were younger and wrote as often as we should; newspaper clippings of marriages, graduations, and trophies awarded to awkward teenaged athletes and scholars; tattered and care worn birthday cards scrawled by seven-year-old hands and younger; and enough tiny and faded school pictures of gap toothed, tow headed children to fill a large boot box. While the middle drawer contained a veritable archive for Douglas family events and recognitions, it was in the bottom drawer where things became interesting.

Nestled among a better quality of socks, a few nice silk scarves that I had never seen him wear, and an almost full bottle of French cologne, label worn and faded and looking to be close to fifty years old, was an oversized cigar box. The box, worn but still shiny and gold, was covered with vivid paintings of beautiful women and men wearing jewels and elaborates costumes and hats. They were smoking and smiling and engaging one another in dynamic repartee, casting furtive glances across one another's shoulders, sharing secrets, leering and smirking playfully.

One dark and mysterious young Indian gentleman peered across the crowd and into the eyes of a fair-skinned youth who returned his gaze shyly, with a hand held reprovingly to the warmth of his flushed cheek. The characters all but jumped off the box and into my head.

"I'll just take this last load from the closet to my car," Tom called on his way out the door. "Back in a minute."

I grunted a non-committal response.

Alone in the room, the box continued to captivate me and I ventured to open it. Though nothing shocking lay hidden within its contents, I was keenly aware that I had never before seen anything in the box in my life. Several flowers, pressed between tissues and brown about the edges; a ticket stub to the Paris Opera; labels soaked and removed from bottles of wine then glued onto yellow and waxen paper; a bundle of letters, addressed in a fine hand and tied with a pale purple ribbon. There was a cross on a simple chain of soft yellow gold curled in the corner of the box next to another silky scarf of paisley, deep burgundy, and green. And a small photograph. Within an elaborately gilded frame, embellished with beautiful hand carved fruits and mythical creatures, the subject of the photograph was a woman, English or American likely. Her hair was twisted up and her face was faded and pale to the point of striking me odd. I examined the photo and turned the frame over in my hand. A small clasp easily moved on the back of the frame allowing it to open like a book. I flipped at the clasp several times with my forefinger and watched it rotate around on its spindle before I let the tiny door fall open and reveal what, if anything, was hiding inside. And there it was. A stunning photograph of a young and beautiful French man, dark skinned with wavy hair, deep warm eyes, a hint of a smile.

He looked out at me from the photograph and clutched me by the heart.

There, within his eyes, was the answer to every question we had ever had about our beloved Uncle Flu; the savior of our family; the strongest man in our lives. And written across the bottom of the photo, in a loving and elegant hand, were the words, "To My Fluellen - For the love that will always be. Yours, Jules."

Tom and Henry stuck their heads back in the door. "About through?" they called.

I cleared my throat and wiped a sleeve across my eyes. "Another minute," I answered hesitantly. "Wait on me out front?"

As the cousins' footsteps echoed quieter down the corridor, I closed the frame and slid it into my shirt pocket. The remainder of the things I lifted into the box, stood and, without even a last look about the room, turned, flipped the light switch to off, and shut the door, leaving the room behind.

Momma

My momma could see the pain in a person's soul the
way some folks see a stain on a patchwork quilt. Hidden
sometimes amidst the patterns and the texture of the weave,
next to a pretty little piece of calico or a rough old corduroy
square. Waiting there on a keen eye to catch it unaware and
then never look at it again without the shame of the knowing
it's there. Momma called it sighting. She said sighting was
like looking into a misty rain. A person could stand in front
of her and a feeling she could see, like a fine spray, would
come down and outline their body. It'd hover around the
person in swirling colors, pinks and golds, close to the skin.
Moving as the person moved like sharp morning sunlight
slipping through the trees at the edge of the woods. It was
in that outline that Momma could sight. She could tell what
somebody kept inside. Tell their secret. Everybody had one
at some time or another, Momma said. A secret or a pain.
Something festering dark and deep near the core of their soul
that needed the curing powers of the wind and the bleach of
the light of the day. It's what makes us real, Momma used to
say. And bringing it to light, well, that's what we're here for.
That's what Momma said.

It would take a while for Momma to draw out what
was in some people. And when she did, the truth often only
rolled off their hips or floated up from their ankles to waft
away into the air. For others, pain just pure sprang off of

their shoulders like rain bouncing back from an old tin roof. It gushed from the palms of their hands and beamed off their chests, begging to get out. I'd see Momma looking, her pearly blue eyes running up and down the skeleton of a person that she could see on the outside of their skin. She'd pull the long grey braid that hung down her bent back around to the front of her high-collared dress and stroke it, like a child rubs an old barn cat. Before long, sure as the world, she'd draw back, quick-like. I'd know then that she had it. She had the sight.

Sometimes, Momma would look away once she had sighted somebody. She'd start talking about how purple her hydrangeas were that year and wondering if her flower beds had too many pine needles in them or maybe they didn't have enough. Or, she'd make an excuse, say she had to go and put on a pot of stew beef for supper or make a pan of biscuits. Other times though, the words would burst right out of her. She'd say things that seemed to reach down into a soul and break away every thread they had that was holding what was in them together. Matter not, people were always drawn to Momma like sweaty children to a muddy pond and tired old men to a sturdy fence post. They couldn't help it.

I was Momma's only child, a change of life baby. We spent a fair amount of time together, even after I was grown and married to Jay Thomas with a baby of my own. We'd sit on her wide-slatted front porch and snap beans to the sound of baby Jean cooing and bees buzzing in and out of the yellow lilies that grew by the rails of her stoop. Momma would complain about her stiff joints and how Daddy had to line up the dilly beans just so in the mason jars before he'd put them in the canner. I'd listen and wonder when I'd have the nerve to complain about my Jay Thomas like Momma did about Daddy.

"He's a persnickety old peckerwood," she'd fuss, filling the well she'd made in her gingham apron with runner beans from a splintered bushel basket set between our

64

straight back chairs. Beans from hers and Daddy's garden, long and slender, like her fingers, and so juicy green they'd spit on your face when you snapped them and you could taste their sweetness when the spray hit your tongue.

"I guess I was given him to keep me in line," she'd finally say, crooking her mouth into a sideways smile and winking at baby Jean, cooing with the bees.

We'd heard tell of the Martins and even seen them from a distance before we actually met them that day in the church parking lot. Seen them standing in front of Diller's Hardware Store talking to Mr. Diller; Mr. Martin's palms turned up to the blue of the sky and waving around in circles with every word he spoke. He was the new minister of music at the Methodist church and was making the rounds meeting folks in town. Miz Martin, his wife, was looking in the picture window at Diller's at the canners and the Ball jars while the men talked. She seemed fancy, that day in town. A lot of make-up. Real nice blue dress. No children.

Next Sunday, it was Mr. Martin who came walking toward where we'd parked the pick-up trucks in the shade of the shaggy bark hickory nut trees by the cemetery gate. Jay Thomas and Daddy were talking to some men about bass fishing, and Momma was wandering through the headstones, whispering to people she'd known long ago, and making her way to Grandma Jeannie's plot with a bundle of lemon verbena from the yard. Preaching was over.

Momma disappeared around the corner of the old tool shed and headed back toward where Aunt Agnes was buried. She'd be gone a while, once she got to visiting. I bounced Baby Jean on my hip and blew cool breath under the brim of her yellow lace bonnet to ease the rash the July heat had brought on. Honeysuckle was thick in the air. Mr. Martin walked in long steps toward me, swinging his lanky arms with a crook in his elbow, his big hands flying out to the side of him like a rooster strutting in the sand.

"How do," he said, squeezing my fingers with a hand already sweaty from shaking so many others at the end of the service. His hair was cinnamon red and a dark pink flush peeped through the freckles on his cheeks and ears. He was a big man. Tall, and wide across the chest in a way that was not quite fat, but was big enough still to cast a shadow on both the baby and me.

"You must be Odette Lavender's girl. Iz'zat right?" His voice had a sweet, sticky twang to it that hung in the air a little too long. Sounded like Tennessee, to me.

"Yes sir," I said, shifting the baby in my arms and looking toward Jay Thomas's circle of men that had moved out to the edge of the parking lot to survey a field of soybeans growing on down the road. They had dove hunting on their minds.

"I been hearin' yo' momma's the one I need to know if I'm gonna get me any good peach preserves this year," Mr. Martin said smiling, his green speckled eyes floating around the rusty old pick-up like he was looking for something he'd lost and thought I might know where to find it.

"You know how to cook like yo' momma?" he asked, turning his chin down so his eyes came at me straight on, as if he were asking a serious question.

"Yes sir, a bit," I said. "She puts clove in 'em."

"Clove?" he squinted his eyes a bit harder.

"In the preserves," I answered, reminding him of his question. I didn't wait for him to respond.

"Momma's visitin' grave sites right now."

He took out a starched white handkerchief from his pocket and wiped the dirty sweat from his forehead then turned, shook his head, and waved to the woman sitting in the front seat of a long, shiny grey car, the color of the snaps on Jay Thomas's overalls.

"My wife," he said, tossing his head back in her direction. Her chin was down and I couldn't make out anymore about her then than I could the day we passed them on the street. The heat was coming off the hood of their car in little spirals. I waved, but she didn't see.

"It might be a while on Momma," I said. "They's a lot of our people ..."

"Mr. Martin?" Momma's voice behind me made me jump. She came around the front of Daddy's truck and laid her white patent leather purse and Grandma Jeannie's verbena, still wrapped in wet brown paper, on the pick-up's blistering hood. She held out her spotted hand.

"Miss Odette," Mr. Martin said, taking Momma's hand slower than he'd taken mine and not squeezing it nearly as tight. He opened his mouth to say something, but let his jaw hang there, as if he'd just woken up from a deep sleep and couldn't figure out whether he was still dreaming or not. He reached for the hanky in his pocket again, the shine from his gold wedding band catching the glint of the sun and bouncing into both mine and Momma's eyes. He wiped at his face.

"I been meanin' to meet you, Miss Odette ...," he said apologetically.

Momma wrapped her left hand around Mr. Martin's wrist and pulled down on it a little until his wide shoulder was stooped and she could see well into his face.

"Them was purty songs today," she said slowly, squinting at a spot just above his head, like she could see clean into his skull.

Mr. Martin cocked his head to one side and made a face like he had just been told something he'd rather not have known. He tried to look away from Momma's eyes. Anywhere else. At the silver locket Grandma Jeannie had given her before she died. At the little hat of purple straw with dried lavender and sage from her own patch tucked into the band. At the crocheted lace collar of her pink Sunday dress. But his eyes went right back to Momma's.

"I ... I 'preciate that, ... Miss Odette," he said, his words starting to rattle and catch.

Momma pulled him closer.

The voices of the men dwindled to a low rumble. Baby Jean rested her little head against my neck and breathed a slow, sleepy breath. Blue birds chirped in the cedar boxes the Sunday school classes had nailed to the hickory nut trees, and a gusty breeze whipped at the tops of the loblollies above the dusty church yard. I waited, watching Momma's eyes travel all over the border of where Mr. Martin's body met the earth and the sky. She followed his contour, around his wide shoulders and up to the top of his crew-cut head. He stayed put, his hand affixed to Momma's like an old hound dog tethered to a backyard tree. Momma's gaze shifted back to the outline of Mr. Martin's heavy arms covered with a fine poplin shirt, sticky with the heat of the morning and the message of the Lord, and came to rest on the meaty hand she held in her own. Heat rose off the roof of the truck as Grandma Jeannie's flowers wilted in the sun. Momma reached for Mr. Martin's left hand and examined it closely. Palm up. Palm down. She was almost done.

When it happened it sounded as if the life had been kicked out of my momma. A "hoah!" noise that was less voice and more the deep tone of air being forced from the depths of a body fast and hard and mighty. Momma grabbed her stomach, then moved her hand to her face and covered her mouth and nose. Mr. Martin's chin dropped to his chest, his face squeezed into a tight purple wrinkle. He drew in a long, quivering breath and held it. It was no use. At first the tears just trickled, then started coming faster than a summer downpour. The men from the circle looked toward the sound of Mr. Martin's wailing as the preacher stood still on the steps of the church and a quiet came over the whole yard that not even the bluebirds were willing to break.

The breeze rose too high to feel.

"Where is she?" Momma finally asked, her breath coming hard, her head shaking from side to side. She still held his hand, her wide blue veins bulging out between the brown spots and the scars. Daddy's yellow gold wedding band on her middle finger pressed sharply into Mr. Martin's flesh and pinched it to the bone on the side of his trembling hand.

"Where's she at?" Momma said again and louder.

Mr. Martin pulled his body back. Sweat dripped off the point of his chin as the sun beat down harder and harder and the wind stood so still I could feel myself pushing heavy air out of the way if I so much as moved. He tried to clear his throat.

"She's in the car," he whispered.

Momma let his hand fall and hang at the end of his sleeve. His face turned back to the dusty parking lot sand where a steady stream of tears and sweat dripped like dark brown freckles and disappeared into the earth. Momma moved toward Daddy's truck and picked up her purse and Grandma Jeannie's flowers. Then, with the walk of an army, she carried herself and all that was truthful and good across that parking lot dirt to the big grey car where Miz Martin sat sweltering in the summer sun. She stood outside the car and waited, patting her foot, while the wind picked up again and a storm started to mix in the trees. She stood there, hands on her broad hips, braid pinned in a wide rope coil at the nape of her neck, and looked at the woman through the blue tinted windows of the car. Slowly, Miz Martin creaked the door open and carefully pulled herself out.

She was pain, through and through. I could see it in the way she held her elbows in her hands and hugged an emptiness close to her belly. Her neck was stiff as a broomstick and her shoulders were hunched and tight like there was nothing left inside her but a place to hurt some more. She wore a man's long-sleeved white cotton shirt over a little lavender shift. And sunglasses, sunglasses so big they covered any pretty her face had ever known. She'd tied a kerchief, purple with tiny red flowers on long green stems, in a knot under her chin, and pulled it down low. She looked tired.

Momma went to her and gently reached for the
big man-sized sleeve and pushed it up to expose an elbow,
twisted and swollen and blue. Four long purple bruises lay
flat against her wrist like tines on a rake. New blue bruises
mixed with old ones turned to brown and green. On her
shoulder, the print of a man's hand, a big man's hand, looked
to be gripping her still.

Momma felt under the placket of her own Sunday
dress and pulled out a white lace hankie and held it folded in
her open hand. Miz Martin stared at it a minute before she
took it. She pulled the plastic glasses off her face and, even
through pressed powder thick as a winter quilt, the stains on
her cheeks and her eyes and around their sockets, like the
juice of crushed blackberries, shown clear as day. She pressed
the cloth to her nose.

They stood there a minute, Momma and Miz Martin,
and let the sun shine on it all for the world, and the church,
and the hunting and fishing men, and anybody who wanted
to, to see. The wind was working hard by then, swirling up
dust from the lot into little funnels then carrying them away
till they smacked into the trees at the edge of the woods and
fell back to the ground they came from. Momma motioned
for me to crank up Daddy's truck. She put her arm around
Miz Martin's waist and walked her over toward the truck
where they both climbed in.

I threw the stick shift in reverse and whirled the rat-
tling old thing around to bring Momma's side up to where
Mr. Martin still stood, staring at the rut between his wingtip
shoes. Reaching her arm out into the sun and the wind and
the first few drops of a summer shower, Momma handed him
the wilted verbena for Grandma Jeannie's grave.

Solo

There was no end to the stories about Solo's momma's pies, as far as Solo was concerned. Pecan, deep-dish peach, buttermilk chess; everybody had a favorite. But the legacy of how to make Momma's pies was a gift Solo had yet to inherit. Leave it to Netty, her snit of a cousin, to sucker punch that message right into Solo's tender and unmarried belly.

Aunt Mae had *so loved* Momma's blackberry cobbler, Netty had whimpered from the funeral parlor porch. Couldn't Solo help her momma make *one last cobbler* to share with the family *one last time* before they sent Aunt Mae off to glory? Netty's voice dripped with molasses as she batted her stubby eyelashes at Solo and dabbed a tissue beneath her nose.

A steady stream of organ dirge captured Netty's words like a puddle does rain and the next thing she knew, Solo was rifling through her momma's kitchen cabinets searching for a recipe for cobbler and a bit of the confidence she'd lost since flying home from college up North.

Solo heard the soft hum of her momma's snore as it vibrated above the radio and wafted down the hall. The rocking creak of her sitter's chair kept an odd beat.

It had been so long since Momma had fried pies and rolled out biscuits in her kitchen that disorder was now mixed in amongst the utensils and pans. Little foil packets of ketchup and paper sachets of salt littered the drawers that had once meticulously aligned rolling pins, pie tins, and spoons. Solo sniffed the air for the memory of pound-cake or sweet

71

potato pie, and got nothing but the scent of her own stale coffee in a paper carry-out cup.

Reaching toward a dusty shelf high above the sink, Solo fetched a fat cookbook that opened in a flurry of clippings and papers. Newspaper articles of engagements, wedding photographs, and birth announcements floated to the Formica like blossoms from a dogwood tree.

Solo stared at the collage of her cousins' lives, a scrapbook of the birthright she'd abandoned, and felt the weight of the disappointment she had visited upon Momma slide over her shoulders like a leaden shawl. With no sister to share the yoke of tradition, Solo had felt overwhelmed by Momma's expectations; unsuited, if not unfit, to meet the demands of marriage and the mysteries of maternity. Academics were her escape; a shelter to steal guiltily behind when her family's definition of womanhood called.

Giving up the search, Solo sent the sitter home for the night, slipped into her momma's room and perched on the edge of her bed. She looks so small, Solo thought, eyeing the outline of her mother's body under the covers. Her anxiety mounted as she contemplated the challenge of creating from scratch a masterpiece like the ones her mother had come to be known for. What kind of culinary magic could be taught at this late stage of the game?

Taking the dried blossom of her momma's hand tenderly into her own, Solo watched her squint milky eyes into the drawing dusk.

"Momma," she heard herself saying, "I need to make a pie."

Momma blinked.

"Blackberry cobbler for Aunt Mae's wake."

Momma's voice was tiny; barely static in the air.

"First, …"

Solo moved her face closer to her Momma's words.

"Take a can of biscuits …"

Solo sighed.

Desport

Desport Dreher adjusted the hooks on his overalls as he stood on the rickety steps of his front porch waiting on enough day break to see his way clear to the barn. Already, a mist floated across the fields that spread out before his eyes, watery and foggy with a thick morning film. New day clouds glimmered in soft streaks of light that peeked over the edge of the piney woods, loblolly and long needle, that blocked the wind off Desport's field of hay. Another light, shadowy and moving with the heat of the stove that had cooked his sausage and eggs for breakfast, burnished through four window panes from the kitchen and lay on the peeling gray paint of the front porch slats.

Damn overalls, bigger on him every day, stretching in the wash until they near about didn't fit, Desport thought. He fumbled with the metal fasteners and the stringy cloth, shot through with sticks from diaper pins once used to extend the length of his straps in the days when Maggie made so many fried apple pies, so many buttered biscuits, that nothing he put on in the mornings was roomy enough for the comfort of his belly.

"Lookit you, Ol' Man," Maggie used to say, patting his fat stomach with the palm of her wrinkled hand. "We got our young 'un grown up and you about to take over her job. You keep growin' and we'll have to get you a new wardrobe," she'd laugh and stand on the tip of her toes to kiss him lightly on the brown spots and spidery red veins that spattered across his shiny forehead. She'd wipe her hands on a thin terry cloth apron and go back to her work, rolling out biscuits with a hard maple pin and punching them into circles with a warped biscuit cutter.

73

"You put it on the table," Desport would grumble to his wife and notice how the wisps of her blond gone gray hair curled at the nape of her neck, no matter how many pins she put in her bun and that, just beneath, where her neck met the soft collar of her calico summer dress, tiny hairs, still blond, still tender and fine, lay soft like fur on a newborn pup.

The screen door slammed behind him and Margaret, always hurrying Margaret, kissed her daddy on the cheek then clip-clopped down the steps in black leather pumps and a skirt too short for Desport's liking.

"I'll be a little late coming out to fix supper," she said over her shoulder as she climbed into the low-riding car and balanced a cup of coffee, poured from the percolator in her parents' kitchen into a flat-bottomed mug, on the dashboard. "I've got a meeting at the bank after work."

"Don't hurry," Desport called after her, waving the stronger of his hands.

"There's sausage biscuits wrapped in tin foil on the stove top for dinner. Eat you an apple and some Fig Newtons," she shouted out the window as the car drove the half loop that made a driveway in front of the clapboard house. Desport waved again. Margaret stopped the car by the mailbox and turned to blow him a kiss.

"Did you hear what I said, Daddy?" she called back from the widow of the idling vehicle.

"I hear," he answered, turning his head to look toward the tree line in the distance. The red tail lights disappeared around the curve in the country road that marked the spot where Desport's property ended.

The air turned a shade of blue-gray and lavender as dawn settled in, and the stumps and shrubs in the yard were more comfortable to Desport's eyes. Time was, he could walk every inch of his property in the dark and never stub a toe. Many was the pitch black night that he wandered out to the farthest barn to check on Margaret's horse, Dolly, ready to foal or frightened by the thunder of a coming storm. Often times, he'd slip out to the clothes line to take in the sack of clothes pins Maggie had left hanging on the line, lest they rust in the rain he smelled surely on its way. Still, in his mind's eye, he could see it all; tell where every bulb was planted, where every bluebird put her next. He could walk his property and hang his tools on nails in the walls of every shed on his land.

In his mind, he could.

But accommodating the left side of his body as it had gone slow on him, negotiating the way it made him cheat to the side when he tried with all his might to walk a straight line, had completely turned Desport around. Maggie was the first to notice.

"Desport Dreher, what are you up to out there? Come into the house for supper, she called out the screen of the open kitchen window. Desport smelled the pepper from fried chicken as it mixed with the acrid tang of vinegar Maggie added to her turnip greens in a big black pot on the stove.

"I'm fixin' to wash the mud off my boots and fill ol' Cat's pan with water, if I can get past these danged azaleas of yours," he answered in an aggravated voice. "They need trimmin' back."

Maggie stopped stirring the greens, the wooden spoon motionless in her hand.

"What's the matter with you, Old Man?" she spoke, softer still from behind the red checked curtain in the kitchen. "The spigot's back yonder beneath the bathroom window." She waited and listened, hearing only the raspy intake and release of her husband's breath. "Don't you mess up my azaleas," she teased and her lips pressed tight and thin one against another.

In a while the shrubs rustled against his pants legs and Maggie heard the metallic squeak of the faucet handle at the back of the house, then a gush of water as he rinsed out the cat's pan.

"Desport?" she called out and waited for him to answer.

"Desport?"

"I'll be indirectly," he finally said, in a voice she knew from sorry nights after embarrassing arguments, mistakes made over years of growing up and growing old together.

The sun, a half ball of intense gold now, bathed the yard as Desport descended the steps one at a time, leaning on the worn smooth railing that gave a memorized inch with the daily pressure of his weight. Stopping first at the rose bed, he tweaked the green reeds, squeezing the plants gently, feeling for life. He pulled back mulched oak leaves and pine straw to expose black earth for the new April sun to warm. The ground was cool and wet beneath his knees as he knelt and, one by one, tended to each of the nineteen rosebushes, one for every Mother's Day since Margaret's girl Peggy was born.

The first year it was a whim, a wooden crate of reedy bushes bundled up in brown paper by the cash register at Canady's Feed and Seed. Assorted colors, twenty-five cents, the sign said. He picked out a healthy-looking plant and put it on the counter by his sack of colored butter beans and the block of suet Maggie had asked him to fetch to put in a feeder outside their newborn grandbaby's window at Margaret's house in town.

"You reckon you can make this thing grow into something," he asked, dropping the wet bundle on the kitchen counter by a load of strawberry preserves cooling in half-pint Mason jars. The thick, sweet smell of strawberries in sugary syrup floated to the roof of his mouth. Peck baskets of berries sat waiting to be washed by the door. Bowls of them drained in the scrubbed clean whiteness of the cast-iron sink, giving off a pink glass glow.

Maggie pushed a lock of hair out of her eyes with a freckled forearm and examined the package, turning it first one way then another. She was sweaty from the steam of the enameled canning pot and her cheeks flushed rosy beneath tiny lines and creases that grazed the far corners of her face. Suddenly her eyes went ablaze. Her face contorted and tears commenced in a flood. She wrapped her thin arms around her husband's neck and, standing on high toes, buried her head in his dusty chambray shirt. Desport put his hands on her shoulders and felt them shudder with sobs as be looked about, studying for a clue. His mouth opened with intent, but only the helpless air of his breath escaped. When her grip loosened he pulled her back and stared at the tear-stained cheeks, the swollen eyes, wiping away the wetness with the side of his rough hand.

"Maggie, I ..."

"Oh Desport," the woman sighed and bit her quivering lip. "You never brought me roses before."

He planted the stalk on early Sunday morning, and they bloomed a pale pink the whole spring and summer through. And every year since, he planted rose bushes a plenty in that same little bed on Mother's Day Sunday mornings, no matter who rode by looking disdainfully at him on their way to preaching at the church.

Leaning on the basin of the concrete birdbath, Desport drew up his weight into a crooked stance, planting both feet for balance and brushed the muddy dew from his knees. The ornate fixture still looked new and out of place in the yard, moss and ivy just this spring starting to climb up the pedestal toward the place where robins bathed. It was rough and cool against his chapped hands. Peggy had used her baby-sitting money to buy the birdbath for her grandmother on the Mother's Day of her 16th birthday. When Peggy was little, Maggie used to say that if a robin redbreast chirped outside her granddaughter's bedroom window, that she, too, could hear its song all the way out in the country, sure as the world.

"Grandma! Grandma! Did you hear it? It was there this morning! Did you hear it?" Peggy cried, jumping out of her mother's still-coasting car to rush into the cool, clean house and find her grandmother pumping her feet at the black wrought-iron pedal of a Singer sewing machine. "Grandma, did you hear the robin?"

Pushing the ladder back chair far enough away from the machine to make an accommodating lap and pulling the cotton curtain fabric from beneath the dust of the eight-year-old Peggy's sneakered feet, Maggie patted her knees. The girl climbed into the cozy nook her grandmother made with her body and snuggled close.

"Did it sound like this?" Maggie asked and she pursed her lips and closed her eyes with deepest concentration. The music floated up and over Peggy's smiling face and wafted out the window on the breeze. Peggy dug the crown of her silky head into a soft place between her grandmother's chin and chest and blew a soundless melody from her own pink lips.

Desport stood in the doorway between the kitchen and the tiny sewing room where his wife had stitched everything from Margaret's baby clothes to her wedding dress. He listened to the two and their song. His own arms itched to scoop up the little girl, to feel her skinny arms around his neck, and throw her bony, scabby knees across his shoulders for a bumpy ride to her playhouse in the barn. He waited though. He waited and he watched and he marveled at the sight the two of them made. Freckled faces, deep caramel eyes that shot twinkles back and forth reflecting one off another like stars in a silvery ocean and the sparkle of the sea on a clear blue night.

More than her mother, Peggy was of the same warp and woof as Maggie. The same details in a bit of Queen Anne's Lace picked by the side of the road that touched Maggie deep enough in her heart to bring on a tear, also made her granddaughter's face go radiant, so contented, so at awe with the particulars of the world.

Peggy tucked her stringy blond head back under Maggie's chin and felt the beat of her grandmother's heart as it kept rhythm with her whistled robin's tune, and Maggie swayed her knees slightly back and forth, her eyes closed but glistening at the lashes. Desport turned and tiptoed out the

front door, gently catching the screen by the tips of his calloused fingers to keep it from slamming shut.

Shadows were stretching tall against the one gray barn
that Desport mostly still used as he swung open the door
with a squeak and felt the gust of cold damp air and smelled
the fertile, fragrant scent of black earth pressed hard on the
floor. He reached for a galvanized pail on the top shelf of the
north side and pried off the lid of a heavy mixture of sun-
flower seeds, millet, and wheat. The smell made him think of
oatmeal and pecan meats, shelling hot roasted peanuts on the
back porch on cool autumn nights while first Margaret and
then, years later, little Peggy climbed the swaying limbs of the
green apple tree that grew by the well.

He moved his loose change from his right overalls
pocket to his left, then pulled out a Case knife and a clean
white handkerchief. Spreading the handkerchief open across
the bottom of an upturned bushel basket, he scooped from
the bucket a good-sized pile of seeds, then gathered the
corners of the cloth together, tied them loosely in a knot and
shoved the bundle back into his right front pocket along with
his knife.

Moving toward the house, the ring of the telephone
sounded from the back screened door, at first almost indis-
cernible from the prattling birds gathered in the hickory nut
trees that led from house to barn to barn. Its ring peeled
louder. He motioned for it to go away with both hands par-
tially raised.

A spigot on a cold metal pipe, wrapped tight with
tape and insulation, stuck up from the ground bringing cool,
fresh well water to Desport's dry lips and stale mouth. Leaning over the water's stream, Desport let it splash on his face
and, removing his canvas hat, turned his forehead into the
flow. Rising up, the water ran down his neck to the back of
his shirt, giving him a shudder that shook him to the tips of
his toes. He thought about the cold biscuits and spicy sausage patties wrapped in a foil envelope waiting between the

eyes of Maggie's grease-splattered stove. Though the juices in his mouth made him think he might want them, the idea of chewing the meat and bread made his stomach turn sour. Swallowing was not as easy a thing to do since Maggie was gone.

Desport reached the bent chinaberry tree and the nearly empty bird feeder he had hung from it outside the window where he and Maggie used to sleep. Yellow gingham curtains moved slightly against the bedroom window as a breeze swept through the house. He could hear the sound of Maggie's sleeping breath, in and out, in and out, as the same breeze moved through the trees above him. Desport took his nights on the front room couch now, no longer able to tolerate the coolness that met his feet when he dare let them slip to the other side of the double brass bed.

He took a seat on the sun-warmed wooden bench by the tree. Bickley's boys from down the road would be coming his way any day now to start cutting and baling hay for him, Desport thought to himself as he slowly poured the feed into the plastic cylinder, spilling not a single seed. Best to get these jobs done while he could.

He hung the full container, four ports pointing toward the bedroom window as Maggie had always asked him to do, and sat back down on the bench, his back comfortable against the moss of the tree. He stretched out his legs and crossed his feet at the collar of his boots. A tune from a hymn entered his head and teased him to give it a place and a name. Slowly the music of Maggie's voice took the chorus. That was it. "Softly and tenderly Jesus is calling, calling for you and for me," he remembered, Maggie humming it while she patted on lavender-scented powder at her dressing table and brushed show strokes through he long blond hair.

The telephone rang again. Desport put his palms over his ears and squeezed his eyes into a deep, tight wrinkle that covered his face from brow to chin.

Chance

Bits and pieces of Chance were spread throughout
the five room mill house where she had grown up, like Easter
eggs abandoned by the hunt. A jump rope hung from a
hook by the back door, untouched since fifth grade. Summer
sandals, shoved under the pie chest, no longer fit her woman-
sized feet. Photographs of a freckled child with teeth at vary-
ing stages of snaggle dotted the walls in an unplanned array,
too high by customary standards, grease from fried chicken,
okra, and ham attracting a thick layer of hazy dust to the
glass; a filtered image of a normal child, a happy childhood.

The surreptitious sounds of early morning kept
cadence with the ticking of the kitchen clock as Chance nego-
tiated the cluttered room, quietly – no need to wake anyone
else. Surveying the pantry, she slipped an unopened jar of
peanut butter into the canvass backpack she had bought
at the Army Navy store at the beginning of ninth grade; a
waxed paper tube of crackers, a box of raisins, an apple from
a chipped yellow bowl.

Momma Nelly's yellow bowl had lived in this house
longer than Chance herself. Most of the kitchen had belonged to Momma Nelly at one time – before Chance's own
momma married at eighteen, a baby girl growing secretly
in her belly, and brought her new husband home to sleep
in the same single bed she had slept in all her life. Momma
Nelly soon learned to tolerate sweet smoke rising off the

back porch and beer cans in her refrigerator – the screen door slamming in the middle of the night until one night, it slammed with a purpose that resonated throughout the house. After that, both the smoke and the beer cans disappeared, but her momma took to sadness like a cat to a cardboard box. She hid in it, and slept in it, and pretended the rest of the world wasn't out there for as long as she could.

Sitting at the kitchen table with a bowl of cereal, Chance only had to crane her neck slightly to see down the short hallway to the door to the bedroom where she and her momma had slept until she was almost 11-years-old. One night, when a Baptist social gathering kept her momma out after Chance's bedtime, she awoke to hairy wrists below suit sleeves moving her sleepy body from the bed to the living room sofa. Chance let her body flop like a dead person's as she took in the meaning of being taken from her bed by a man she only vaguely remembered seeing on some Sunday mornings. Eyes squeezed tight against heavy male footsteps moving back down the hall – another door closed again.

On a fall day, when the leaves had long floated to the ground and blown down the avenues to the river at the bottom of the hill, and the mill village wore a particularly exposed look, unable to hide behind pretentions and foliage, Momma Nelly up and died. The house grumbled with the weight of the grieving neighbors, all bearing some form of congealed salad, casserole, or deviled egg. Then, before all the left-overs were eaten, Chance's momma moved into her mother's old room and Chance was alone in a bedroom for the first time in her life.

To her surprise, the room seemed smaller than when she had shared it with her momma. The walls dingier, the accumulation of dead bug bodies in the bottom of the overhead fixture more unsettling, the sounds coming from her momma's new bedroom up the hall more annoying than she had ever heard them before. She lay that night, in the middle of the bed, and tried not to move – to hold still against the earth moving beneath her, the sky above her, both forcing the passage of time. She gritted her teeth and held tight to bundles of bed sheet clasped against her palms and, with every ounce of energy she could summon, she willed immobility for herself and the universe.

When the bedroom door opened she first assumed it was her mother – missing her maybe, unable to sleep in unfamiliar surroundings. The door stood ajar, permitting an unwelcome light from the hallway to fall across the bottom of Chance's bed; and it did not close. Minutes passed and Chance lay still. No mother's hand on her forehead; no hushed kiss on the top of her head. When the door finally closed, Chance turned her face into the pillow and allowed hot tears to saturate the case. It was not the only night she cried.

Purple streaks of a rising sun shone through the kitchen window and, quietly still, Chance rinsed her spoon and bowl and left them in the drainer beside the sink. She smiled at the plastic spoon, molded into the shape of a princess crown, paint having long ago worn away from morning after morning of oatmeal and applesauce and cereal. She reached for the spoon and held it trembling in her hand, her eyes closed against the memories and the reality of what this moment in time meant to her past. To her future.

There was no going back.

Slipping the spoon down the side of her backpack, she swung the strap over her shoulder and stepped from the kitchen door to a path that led as far away from yesterday as possible, on her way to now.

Reeny

Reeny leaned over the cast iron sauce pan and let
the salted steam wash over her throat and up to the tiny and
pristine highways that defined the contours of her face. There
were few smile lines for the moist air to soften and melt away,
but she breathed the mist in deeply and felt it saturate her
sinuses like a needed drug. She bathed in the little cloud until
the roiling liquid below began to hiss and spit. Opening her
eyes, she cleared her throat and, with resignation, dumped
two cups of dry and well-measured Adluh grits into the boil-
ing water. Then, she stirred.

Noises were beginning to creep down from the floor
above; splashing water; stubborn steps; radio music that came
to her like on a journey from the bottom of a large and empty can. A door slammed and the clatter of a shower curtain as
it scraped across its hollow metal rod told her it was time to
place strips of cold bacon in resolute rows along her momma's old black frying pan. She sniffed and smelled the clean,
herbal scent of her daughter's sudsy morning ritual as it drifted down the stairs and then clashed, like thunderheads, with
the buttery bouquet she herself was creating in the kitchen
below. Funny, she thought, how tiny, invisible molecules of
aromas could admit to the things neither she nor her daughter would say aloud. That the heavy black skillet, for example,
shiny with the patina of hundreds of pounds of pork, would
likely pass no further down the family line than Reeny herself.

85

That the girl, whose mother talked on the telephone to her own momma every morning, searched desperately among the faculty at her college, the women in the bookstore, those who wore business suits and blazers, who carried cell phones and briefcases and important papers, searched for another woman – a woman with a job, a woman with a life – with whom she might communicate. Might talk to. Might just sit down and talk to. Reeny poured herself a cup of coffee, let a big black sip splash against the back of her throat, and peeped in the oven to see if her biscuits had begun to brown.

A door opened above.

"*Mother!*" Dori's voice demanded from the top of the stairs, "Where's my black shirt?"

Reeny thought for a moment, her fingertips resting lightly against the hot oven door. "Ummm … Hanging on the bathroom doorknob – under the towel?"

Footsteps move decidedly back down the hallway on the floor above.

"Not *that* one!" Dori was indignant; insulted already and it was barely eight o'clock.

Reeny squeezed her eyes tight and bit her lower lip. She could hear the mounting hatefulness in her daughter's huffing and puffing all the way to the kitchen table where her husband's plate waited to be cleared. "Let me look for it," she sighed, wiping her hands on a faded dish towel and starting up the stairs.

"Don't *bother!*" Dori shot back. Exasperation, this time. "I've got it now."

Reeny stopped on the third tread and listened to the stomping and slamming of an eighteen-year-old near-woman indulging in the emotional maelstrom of a four-year-old child.

"Fine," she exhaled, and turned back to the path that would lead to her kitchen.

The biscuits were ready; tops golden on the edge of the crowns, centers as evenly brown as the back of a doe.

The heat moving from the oven pushed strands of Reeny's hair back from her face and watered her vanilla bean eyes. She smiled at the pan as she pulled it from the oven and laid it on the kitchen counter across hand-painted tiles that never moved. Reeny's biscuit tiles. She'd rescued them from her grandmother's house when a less sentimental cousin had remodeled the old home place and ripped the old and inefficient but, Reeny knew, spirit-laden kitchen apart. It was the winter before Dori was born and Reeny used a tiny ox hair brush to decorate the dirt-red, rectangular ceramic pieces that had once framed the fireplace that warmed the front half, the living half, of her grandmother's house.

Her boy Devon was only four-years-old the winter Reeny painted and waited so long and longingly for her daughter to come. She painted her tiles as Devon played in the kitchen floor, smearing strokes of water onto pastel dotted pages from a book that magically turned the spots and water into colors that ran all over the page. Reeny knew Devon's prognosis by then; had found out, ironically, the same week she'd heard Dori's bird-sized heartbeat as she lay, flat on her back, jelly smeared cold and gooey across her rounding belly, in the obstetrician's office.

Dr. Morley had been around since most of his patients were babies themselves. The tears didn't surprise him at first. Reeny had cried more than four years before when she first heard Devon's heartbeat; a muffled drum – hollow footsteps in an empty house. But this time the confused puddles in her eyes, the sweet and salty trickle, quickly turned to torrents and Reeny gasped and choked out the news, still news even to her own ears, that her first baby, her perfect little boy, was in fact, less than perfect; flawed. So strange, she'd thought at the time, patient giving doctor bad news … uncomfortable for them both. Sobbing so hard she could barely breathe, didn't really want to breathe, Reeny's heart almost dissolved into a mushy puddle that afternoon as she lay open and exposed on a cold examination table, listening to another pulse throb inside her; knowing how soon she would become the rhythm that she heard. Knowing that no matter how much she loved the sound coming from inside her and how much of herself she gave it that, ultimately, it would quieten, hush, and fade into the distance. Early, like the muted timbre of the beating heart at home, building forts and castles out of Lincoln Logs while his mulish blood cells worked resolutely at defying both his body and his momma's prayers. Or later, like the one that lay within her on the table then, sharing her breath and blood. The one that would one day see her momma's inadequacies as the giant gaping pockets of human frailty that they were. The one that would ultimately be offended by the world of things her mother wasn't; would likely defy the things her momma was.

And through it all, Dr. Morley had kept that heartbeat coming. He'd sat right down by Reeny's bare belly and never moved the Doppler from the place where he'd found the sound. While Reeny cried, her baby thrummed. Full, deep and resonant, the new baby's heartbeat echoed under the sound of Reeny's quietening sobs until, thump, thump, thump . . . it was all she could hear. The erratic and involuntary catches in her own breath couldn't drown out the hammer of her new baby's heart. She stopped weeping, wiped her face, and went home to nurse a dying boy while she waited on a brand new baby girl to come out from her; to greet her; and to immediately start breaking away.

Reeny painted the tiles that winter, traveling back in her mind to the days before babies and prescriptions and late notices; back to the days of canvasses, late nights in the studio, reviews of her work and people she didn't know stopping her on the street to say "Hello." Hello to the artist. She missed the accolades; missed the satisfying film thickness of gouache pigment, the scent of mineral spirits and turpentine; longed for the firm pressure in her hand of the graphite stroke as it forced its carbon particles into the interstices of greasy paper; pined for the satisfaction of birthing a vision that had heretofore darted about, crazily and unconfirmed, in her head. So Reeny painted the tiles with a forest full of creatures in acrylic polymers - cerulean blue, strontium yellow, rose madder - some ancient, that had once lived and breathed; others mythical, that never existed at all. But to everyone she gave a name and a story and a lesson about life and death for her dying little boy to love.

Without looking, Reeny's hand found the worn knob of the kitchen drawer, reached in and pulled out a heavy butter knife. With delicate forefinger and thumb, she took hold of the first biscuit by its cap and let the knife separate the flesh, cut through the miracle of the ingredients, the chemistry she had conducted in order to call up the ghosts of Southern women past who gesticulated and sighed and danced every morning in Reeny's biscuit bowl to create the delicate magnum opus, the staple of the southern kitchen counter.

The stick of butter, taken from the refrigerator before the coffee was put on, was soft and sculpted in its dish. A dollop of the creamy gold slid from the knife's blade and crawled between the sheets of the biscuit's bottom and top. Reeny buttered the biscuits one at a time and arranged them spiraling out from the center of a large ironstone plate. The last ones she set aside on an odd saucer and lightly speckled them with a pinch of sugar. She whipped a piece of waxed paper from the tube and wrapped the bread like a birthday present, carefully creasing the folds, then pushed it to the back of the cook-top, between glowing eyes warming pans of grits and eggs.

Dori's bootsteps sounded down the staircase like rolling gunfire. Reeny looked up from the plate and licked her fingers. Dori, quilled by piercings, splayed an assortment of satchels on the table then headed to the cupboard, passing the food that steamed on the counter and stove. She opened the cabinet door and stood, staring into the contents and the empty spaces between the boxes and cans.

Reeny watched the sway of her daughter's hair, once

the color of whipped honey, now dyed to a black that reflected a spectrum of colors like oil in a puddle. She wanted
to sink her hands in it. She wanted to use her fingers as a
comb and pull the fine, baby silk locks back from her daughter's face, massage the girl's tender scalp, use her forefinger
to lightly trace pictures over the cheeks, freckled nose, and
eyelids. She wanted to pull the warm head to her body and
wedge it there - her shoulder a pillow, her face a shawl; wrap
her arms like wings around the young girl, and rock her back
and forth and back again to the days when their affection for
one another was a palpable substance between them; a whole
cloth that stretched as far apart as either of them needed to
go. Her forearms ached with a pain, as intense as a blow to
the belly, to hold the girl – to just hold her tight. A lump like
malachite grew hard and high in her throat.

Reeny took a bite of hot biscuit and felt the slick
steam scorch the roof of her mouth. Hot liquid butter flowed
over her teeth and up through her brain washing along an
unexpected wave of clarity. She shook her head like a puppy
waking from a long, productive nap. She looked at her daughter, examined closely the back of her head, and could see
hidden there the roots of her own sandy blond hair.

"The biscuits are hot," she said to the child, hesitat-
ing, afraid of how small her voice sounded.

Dori tapped the toe of her boot and swung the
cupboard door to hear it squeak. Reeny took another bite of
bread and stepped to the side of the girl so she could better
see her face. She peered at her eyes, squinted and saw buried
there the deep black coffee puddles of her own and, even
deeper, in streaks off from the center of the fresh young
pupils, the dark penny copper of her momma's.

She swallowed.

"I know you won't eat bacon, Honey, but there are
eggs on the stove."

Tap, tap, tap, tap. Reeny felt odd – suddenly out of
place in her own kitchen.

"And grits." She brought the biscuit to her mouth again.

A large exhalation of frustrated breath puffed from the girl's lips. She turned and let her eyes follow the walls of the kitchen as they led around the table, along her mother's back, then back to where she was standing. There was nothing in there that Dori wanted.

"Dori?"

"I'm not hungry," she said, slamming the cabinet door and stomping to the table to get her bags.

None of the girl's satchels were zipped or fastened and in her haste to remove herself from the prying gaze of her mother's walls, she grabbed awkwardly at her bags, sending the contents fluttering to the floor. As she scrambled to gather her things, drawings poured from one bag; prints and lithographs from another. Automatically, Reeny knelt to help collect the work.

"I've got it," Dori said impatiently, crumpling papers and pushing them into their cases as Reeny began mothering the mess her daughter had made.

That was when she noticed. These weren't random notes from senior English or corrected papers from trigonometry. She cocked her head to the side to take in the pieces of art, that she held in her hands – pieces much like those she might have found in her own portfolio not that many years before. "Kandinsky," she whispered to the images as she shuffled through the growingly familiar prints, "Rauschenberg, Picasso's guitar ..."

She licked a smudge of butter from her lips and inhaled sharply, her mind going back to the place in her memories where art was an escape, a road to another world – a world where she belonged and thrived. "Oooh, a Schiele," she exclaimed, her eyes closing with the memory of an almost sensual satisfaction, "... the one with the black hair." She looked up from the floor at her daughter and felt her face flush.

Dori wrinkled her brow into a confused ribbon. The juxtaposition of her mother and art felt foreign. How had she even heard of the artists whose works she held, much less recognize and respond to them?

Reeny gasped before the girl could speak, "Mondrian – his pier and ocean!" She looked excitedly at her daughter, at ease with her feelings and interpretations of the work – comfortable in her knowledge. "You know, this isn't really abstract at all. You can see it, clear as day, right here," she said, thumping the center of the print with the tip of her finger. "The pier – it's these vertical lines here – it sticks right out into the ocean. It's just a grid, see? And this white paint? That's the starlight reflected in the sea." Reeny was lost in the art. She shuffled through more papers and prints while Dori lowered her knees to the cool linoleum floor, gathered a small stack of sketches and handed them to her mother.

"This … is it yours?" Reeny asked, her face lowered to the abstracted and muted lines and figures.

Dori searched the back of her mother's head. "It's … a copy, sort of," she answered.

"Of … *Guernica*?" Reeny rose from the floor and reached for the two sweet biscuits from the back of the stove.

"Of a bit of *Guernica*," Dori said, raising up herself and settling into a seat at the kitchen table. "It's a detail."

Scrutinizing the sketch, Reeny lowered the heavy saucer to the placemat and pulled the waxed paper from the bread. Steam quickly escaped and pulled her daughter's nose and eyes to the hot, sticky masterpieces on the plate.

"The biscuits look good," Dori raised her eyebrows expectantly, but Reeny busily studied the drawing like a map. The mixed aroma of cinnamon and butter teased her belly; her mouth began to water.

"The biscuits, Momma," the daughter said to the artist standing above her. "Can I have a taste?"

ABOUT THE COVER

The cover of *Buttered Biscuits: Short Stories from the South* is taken from a painting by Thomas Crouch commissioned by the author.

Thomas Crouch is a South Carolina artist who studied at the Lorenzo De Medici School of Art in Florence, Italy and the University of South Carolina. His work is represented in galleries throughout the United States and Europe.

Contact Crouch at thomascrouchart.com.

ACKNOWLEDGMENTS

The following stories were originally published as winners of the South Carolina Fiction Project and appeared in *The Post and Courier*, Charleston, South Carolina between 1993 and 2008: "Mary Anne" as "The Proposal," "Aunt Priss" as "Aunt Priss and the Deer," "Precious," "Alvie and Alvin" as "Shoes," "Momma" as "Lemon Verbena," and "Desport" as "Softly and Tenderly." The South Carolina Fiction Project is sponsored by the South Carolina Arts Commission which receives support from the National Endowment for the Arts.

"The Proposal" was also the winner of the Porter Fleming Literary Competition and appeared in *Inheritance*, edited by Jeanette Turner Hospital and published by Hub City Press in 2001.

"Reeny" as "Buttered Biscuits," "Solo" as "Found Pie," and "Toby and Bess" were winners of the Piccolo Fiction Open in 2003, 2004, and 2006 respectively.

"Dobie" was the first place winner of the W. W. Norton Flash Fiction award in 2008.

"Raylene" as "Releasing Raylene" was the winner of the 2009 South Carolina Writers Workshop Quill contest for fiction.

Grateful acknowledgment is made to the above publications and organizations.

ABOUT
MUDDY FORD PRESS

Muddy Ford Press is a family-owned publishing company located in Chapin, South Carolina and dedicated to providing boutique publishing opportunities for South Carolina writers and poets. Contact us at MuddyFordPress.com.

CPSIA information can be obtained at www.ICGtesting.com
Printed in the USA
LVOW06s0946040514

384321LV00001B/40/P